Did she dare g▓▓

Sylvie wanted to go ▓▓▓▓▓▓▓▓▓▓▓around him. He stood and began to pace. Then he went to her...and put his hands on her shoulders.

Sylvie felt the blush start at her neck and rise to her face. This time, when she looked into Hunter's eyes, she saw the flicker of passion that she thought had disappeared.

She swallowed. She was playing with fire with Hunter Semmes. He wasn't like any man she'd ever known.

The air between them superheated. Her response to Hunter frightened her. Just looking into his eyes made her want him. And she'd known him less than a day. It didn't make sense. It went against all of the rules she'd made to protect herself from the harsh realities of life.

She lifted her face and waited for his kiss.

ABOUT THE AUTHOR

Caroline Burnes has added another cat to her menagerie. Chester is a yellow tabby that she adopted in the middle of Hurricane Georges. The cat had been struck by a car and was wandering in an intersection. Caroline and her growing menagerie wish everyone a happy, safe holiday season.

Books by Caroline Burnes

Familiar Christmas
Caroline Burnes

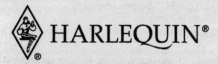
HARLEQUIN®

TORONTO • NEW YORK • LONDON
AMSTERDAM • PARIS • SYDNEY • HAMBURG
STOCKHOLM • ATHENS • TOKYO • MILAN • MADRID
PRAGUE • WARSAW • BUDAPEST • AUCKLAND

For Patti Tierce—who lost an old friend this past year.
Her heart is always open to the love of a kitty.

ISBN 0-373-22542-3

FAMILIAR CHRISTMAS

Copyright © 1999 by Carolyn Haines

Visit us at www.romance.net

Printed in U.S.A.

Broadway

Central
Park

MANHATTAN

Hunter's
Toy Factory

KATZ Meow Toy Store

5th Ave.

34th St.

7th Ave.

CAST OF CHARACTERS

Familiar—The feline detective was in town to do a little Christmas shopping. Now he must help save Christmas!

Hunter Semmes—His invention could help millions of children—if a blackmailer doesn't get it first.

Sylvie West—She's never had a merry Christmas. This year, will Santa deliver the man of her dreams?

Clarise Blalock—She owns KATZ Meow toy store. Would she endanger lives to turn a profit?

Chester Fenton—There's something different about the kindly old man.

Augie Marcel—His sudden appearance connects Sylvie to the blackmailer. But how?

Alice McBride—Sylvie's co-worker becomes her best friend and supporter.

Connie Semmes—Hunter's ex-wife can't seem to stay out of his life.

Peyton Klepp—Is Connie's new fiancé as rich and successful as he seems?

Lila Vernon—She'll break hospital rules to help Hunter. Does she want more than friendship?

Chapter One

When ole Bing crooned about glistening tree tops and sleigh bells in the snow, he was certainly thinking about a Yuletide season like this one. Dig that white stuff. It's coming down in flakes the size of quarters—and tickling the whiskers of one elegant black cat who's on a holiday shopping spree.

There's my destination. KATZ Meow Toy Emporium. The most unusual, finest, most creative toys in the world. A dreamland for the tots. Too bad Jordan couldn't come with me, but if she was here, then her present wouldn't be a surprise.

After helping Molly and Sulle save young Alan last August, my bank account grew by an abundant amount. Those two humanoids were very generous in their contribution to the Familiar retirement fund! The scheme did require a little human intervention, but now I'm the proud owner of a platinum credit card, and I intend to do some damage! Wouldn't Clotilde love to be here with me? Her duties as a Washington feline hostess have held her back in the capitol. Too bad. But I've already found the perfect Christmas gift for her—that idiotic tape of those dogs barking ''Jingle Bells.'' Jeez! Can you imagine the *amount of bad doggy breath that went into that piece of lunacy? All those slobbering mutts willing to do anything to gain approval. That's the perfect definition of dog. With the exception of that old fleabag Ouzo. Now he was a trial, but he was smart. Anyway, every time Clotilde and I hear the doggy "Jingle Bells," we nearly die. Dogs will do anything to get attention. Anything.*

Clotilde told me there's a cat rendition of the Christmas tune, but she and I both agree those must be computer-generated meows. Either that or the felines had been lobotomized. No self-respecting puss would ever perform in such a ridiculous manner.

Well, maybe for a casserole of crabmeat and cheese.

I just finished breakfast and already I'm thinking about food again. Big kitty sigh. Peter picked me up this morning and groaned, as if I weighed too much for him to carry. It was meant as an insult, but it also made me wonder if I don't need to up the exercise program a little. After all, that big Christmas spread is just around the corner and I want plenty of room for the goodies.

I'll worry about a diet tomorrow, to quote one of the smartest women in fiction. Right now I'm at the door of the store. It's opening and I'm going in. With my platinum card around my neck, I am going to shop till I drop.

Man, I just love this place. My special quest is a veterinarian doll for Jordan. The world needs more good animal doctors, and she shows a real talent for nurturing the wee creatures. She's only five, but there's no time like the present to start training a humanoid. They are rather slow to learn, God love them. Jordan is smarter than most, but she needs direction. And I'm the perfect person to give it to her.

Look at all the decorations! This place is a fantasyland. And check out the legs on that Santa's helper. Big wolf whistle here. If Santa had her in his workshop he'd never make it to deliver the presents. She is one raven-haired knockout.

I'm not really interested in the toddler toys she's stocking the shelves with, but I'm not averse to doing a little window shopping—especially when my primary view is those long, magnificent legs in cute little tights. And I think Eleanor should buy herself one of those daring elf outfits. I love that shade of green, and the jagged hemline—mama mia is that hot!

Here comes Santa. But this is odd. He's sweating and looking around like he thinks the Mafia has put a hit out on him.

Hey! Hey buddy! He's grabbing the sack of toys from my elf. Holy Christmas! Now he's grabbing my elf! And he has a gun! The man is abducting one of Santa's helpers. This is a job for Familiar, supersleuth.

While his back is turned I'll just slip into the bag of toys. Won't he get a surprise when he opens the sack!

THE PACKAGING of the Molly McBright and Buster Bigboys was exceptional, Sylvie West thought as she arranged the toys on the designated shelf. Like every other toy in the world's most famous children's store, these two creations were just perfect. And delivered late. There'd been some holdup on the shipping order that she didn't understand. She'd only heard gossip

among the store employees that the inventor of the
dolls was a kook and at the last minute tried to re-
claim his shipment. She'd heard he even offered to
pay double what the store had paid for the dolls. That
did a lot for his credibility!

When that failed he'd demanded the dolls be tested
for a virus or bacteria. Of course the guy was some
kind of paranoid nut—New York City abounded with
brilliant people who were just unable to cope in society. The dolls had been rigorously tested. Nothing
was found and the end result was that she was working like a fiend to get the toys on the shelves in time
for the holiday shopping stampede.

They were cute though. She held the Buster and
squeezed him again. Perfect for wrapping and putting
under the Christmas tree to bring cries of delight and
pleasure from thousands of toddlers.

At the mental image of a beautiful tree all decorated with family ornaments, children in their pajamas reaching for beautifully wrapped gifts, a fire
blazing in the background and carols playing gently
on the radio, Sylvie wanted to throw up. It was all
such a crock. That was the Christmas designed and
packaged by the advertising gurus of Madison Avenue. It had nothing to do with what Christmas really
was—one big disappointment year after year.

She reached into the bag and pulled out another
Buster Bigboy. The soft-form doll was sort of cute.
She pressed a thumb on the plastic wrap and felt the
almost-human flesh. Whoever invented that substance was ingenious. Toddlers would love to hold
it, squeeze it—and chew on it. That's why the little
doll was filled with a new antibacterial substance and

small doses of herbal vaccines and vitamins to boot! A toy that delivered a good time and good health.

She carefully put Buster on the shelf, making sure the arrangement was attractive. That was her job, to make Christmas even more appealing.

It was simply the cruelest irony of her life that she was working as a Santa's helper in a store that made Christmas the ultimate shopping holiday of the year. She glanced down the aisle and saw a family that had come from Japan simply to experience Christmas in the Big Apple and to shop at this toy store for their lucky children. Judging by the expression on the faces of the two beautiful girls, it was a fantasy come true.

Sylvie kept stocking the shelf, but she surreptitiously watched the happy family. The little girls were still young enough to believe in Santa Claus— she could see that clearly on their faces as they pointed at toys and told their mother that the beautiful stuffed giraffe should be added to the list for Santa.

"Bah! Humbug!" Sylvie whispered to herself. Old St. Nick was one of the cruelest jokes ever played on children. These little girls were the lucky ones. But what about the kids who would wake up Christmas morning with nothing? No tree, no stocking, no big lunch. Just a big fat zero and a load of disappointment and guilt that they hadn't been good enough for Santa to visit. What about those kids? Christmas would be one big heartbreak.

She jammed another Molly McBright onto the shelf with such force that she sent ten toppling to the floor. Damn it all, why hadn't she gotten a job as a paralegal? At least the law was a reality she appreciated.

She saw the Santa coming down the aisle toward her—a tall man in a poorly fitted Santa suit, his whiskers askew. She frowned. If he was going to play the part, he could at least do it properly. He looked as if he'd flunked out of Santa school.

She opened her mouth to speak just as she saw the sweat on his forehead and the fevered look in his eyes. Something was wrong with him, and it was obvious enough to halt her in her tracks.

"Put the toys back in the bag," he said, grasping her toy sack with one hand while the other pointed a deadly looking gun at her.

Sylvie started to say something but found that her vocal cords were frozen. Her gaze was fixated on the gun, and her limbs were paralyzed.

"Get busy," he said in curt tone. "Now!"

To her surprise she felt her arm draw back and her hand fist up. Before she could stop herself, she took a swing. Santa stepped back and she found herself clutched firmly against his chest, his arm so tight around her waist that she thought she'd faint from lack of oxygen.

Tarnation! Now this was truly what she needed during the holiday she hated more than anything else in the world!

HUNTER SEMMES was as surprised as everyone in KATZ Meow when he found his right arm around the waist of a scantily clad Santa's helper and his left arm burdened with a sackful of toys. The gun he also carried was rendered virtually useless, but in the crowd of terrified mothers, screaming children and paralyzed employees, no one seemed to care that he'd had to drop the weapon in with the toys in order to manage everything.

"Clean off the shelf," he ordered the struggling elf. "Put all of the toys back in the bag."

Instead of complying, she tossed her black hair and kicked him in the shin with the heel of her elf boot, which was surprisingly solid.

He moved the sack closer to the shelf and whispered tersely in her ear, "This is no time for a display of bad temper. Put those toys back in the sack and I'll release you." He found it hard to speak clearly through the white fuzz of the fake beard he wore. He also had an urge to sneeze. But he knew if he lost control of the situation, even for a second, all would be lost. To his surprise the woman began to shovel the toys back into the sack.

"I don't know what your problem is, mister, but you're going to regret this."

Hunter was sure that she was right. He already regretted it. But he had no choice. He'd tried every reasonable route under the sun, and no one had listened to him. No one had believed him. In fact, after his demands for testing the dolls and his attempt to buy them back at twice the price KATZ Meow had paid, he was now viewed as certifiably crazy. The police had been very clear when they told him that if he set foot in the store or called them again, *he* would face a list of charges a mile long. He was on the kook list. So he had been forced to resort to stealing the dolls. And the furious elf wasn't helping matters.

He looked down at the woman's beautiful hands— nails a bright red that coordinated her outfit with the season. She was scooping the Molly McBrights into the toy sack. Even as Hunter looked at the beguiling little dolls, he felt the lash of disappointment. He'd had such high hopes for them.

As soon as the shelf was clear, he managed to drag the sack and the wiggling elf toward the door. "Stand back," he called as he made slow progress to the exit. "I don't want to hurt anyone." If they only knew the dangerous weapon in his sack was a water pistol. But that was one of the problems with the toy industry, in his opinion. Even the water guns were so realistic looking they weren't toys any longer.

"You're not going to get away with stealing a sack of toys from the number-one toy store in the world," the elf insisted.

Hunter figured she was right. In fact, it was his plan that he wouldn't get away with it. But the ensuing publicity would alert the public to a grave danger—one that, so far, no one had believed. He wasn't a kook or a fool or some crazy eccentric. Someone had threatened him, and in very clear language had told him exactly what they could, and would, do to his dolls. But it was a phone call. He had no evidence. And when he'd finally forced the authorities to take action and test several of the dolls, all had come out clean. Now he was viewed as another lonely crazy who wanted to spoil Christmas, no matter the personal cost.

He made the doorway, his arm around the slender waist of the woman. His intention was to let her go. When he heard the explosion, he turned, elf still in his arms. Before he could react, a chunk of block exploded from the façade beside him.

Someone was shooting at him! And the woman began to struggle in earnest. She was twisting and turning like a wild thing, her silky hair flying into his face and almost blinding him. He had no choice but to tighten his grip. He felt the pressure of her breasts against his arm.

"Hold still," he urged her.

Another shot sent more of the store's façade splintering. Debris peppered his ear. People milled and screamed.

Hunter was completely unprepared for the soft cry that escaped his captive. Even more startling was the fact that she suddenly went limp in his arms. As her head rolled to one side, he saw the blood rushing from a wound to the side of her forehead. She was injured! Either she'd been shot or a piece of the building had fragmented and struck her.

Hunter swung her into his arms, unwilling to leave her behind. He hefted the sack of toys and ran as fast as he could to the van he'd left waiting on the sidewalk.

Bullets snipped at his heels, but he didn't slow. He launched himself, the woman, and the toys into the van and took off into the fastest moving lane, away from the thick of New York City holiday traffic. Behind him, sirens blared.

SYLVIE CAME TO long enough to realize she was in some moving conveyance, and the ride was not a gentle one. She forced her eyes open and saw the interior of a van. Beside her was the sack of toys, and inside the sack, something moved. In her groggy state, she was more amused than afraid of the lump moving beneath the canvas. Reaching out a hand she pulled the drawstring on the bag. A black cat stuck his head out of the sack and looked at her with wide golden eyes.

"Where did you come from?" she asked.

Her voice made the driver of the van swerve as he looked back at her.

"Lie still and don't move," Santa Claus said to her.

Sylvie had no intention of moving. She was in the middle of her worst nightmare, or perhaps she'd died and gone straight down to the hottest regions of Hades. She hated Christmas. She hated all the seasonal merriment, the shopping frenzy and the hypocritical nature of all the fake good cheer. But more than all of those things combined, she hated Santa Claus. What a fraud he was. Well, he was showing his true colors now. He was nothing more than a thief and a kidnapper!

Even as she thought it, she knew she was not being rational. Why was she on the floor of a van with a black cat patting her gently with one paw? Who was this bearded man who was driving so fast that she rolled around like a sack of potatoes?

"Stop this van immediately," she said as she braced herself against another sharp turn.

Before she could prepare herself, the van entered a tunnel and halted abruptly.

"Glad to oblige," Santa said. "Just lie still."

"As if I'd listen to a kidnapping Santa Claus," she answered, bracing on her hands so that she could sit up. Her head felt as if someone had slugged her with a hammer. What had happened? The last thing she remembered was Santa's strong arm around her waist, hugging her tightly against him as they made a desperate exit out of the toy store. She started to sit up, but the pain in her head was blinding. She lifted a hand to her head, and when she felt something warm and sticky, she knew it was blood.

Then she remembered the gunshots. "I've been shot," she whispered, more shocked than afraid.

Santa climbed into the back of the van and knelt at her side. Beneath the bushy white eyebrows she found brown eyes that were both worried and kind. His fingers moved expertly to her wound. "I couldn't leave you injured," he said as he probed the wound. "I wasn't sure if it was police or someone else shooting at us."

"I wouldn't have been hurt at all if you hadn't kidnapped me," she said, feeling her anger return.

"I'm sorry," he said, his attention focused on her head.

"Let me out of here." She pushed his hand away.

"Easy," he said, pressing her back down and holding her. "It isn't a terrible wound, but you're going to need a few stitches."

"And who's going to provide them?" she asked, angrier than ever that she was too weak to fight him off. She hadn't worked at the store long enough to gain any health benefits. A doctor would cost more than she had at the moment.

"I am," he said with cool confidence. "I'm a doctor," he said, pulling the white beard away to reveal a clean-shaven, square jaw and a handsome face. High cheekbones angled upward, and light, chocolate-colored eyes watched her with concern. Sylvie stared at him. He was good-looking enough to be on the cover of a man's magazine.

HE SAW THE DISBELIEF in her eyes, and then the panic. He could almost hear her thoughts. She was being held hostage by a man who pretended to be Santa Claus and believed he was a medical doctor. No wonder she looked so afraid.

"I'm a pediatrician," he said. "I'm qualified to put in a few stitches."

"Right, Santa. Who's going to assist, Rudolph?"

He sighed. For a woman who looked as sweet as an angel, she was one tough customer. Her edges were sharper than a razor blade, and he wondered what had happened in her life to make her so caustic.

His attention was diverted for a moment as the sound of sirens grew closer. His plan was ruined. He'd never meant to take a hostage, and now he was truly running from the law.

"Let me see about your head," he said, "then you can go."

"You think I'm buying that line?"

"It isn't a line, it's the truth. I never wanted to take you with me, but once you were hurt, I couldn't leave you lying on the sidewalk. Whoever shot at us could have been an excited rookie cop, or someone out to get me—and I couldn't be sure they wouldn't shoot you if I left you."

For a moment he saw a glimmer of acceptance in her china-blue eyes, and he was unprepared for the gut kick of emotion that came with such trust. Then her skeptical nature reasserted itself and the blue turned hard and stormy.

"Right. You didn't intend to take a hostage when you walked into a department store—a children's toy store, I might add—with a gun that looked as if it was taken off James Bond."

"Funny you should say that," he said, feeling one corner of his mouth twitch. "It is a James Bond gun. I bought it at KATZ Meow. Last night—$12.99." Again he saw the flicker of what might be trust. "That's when I hatched this plan to steal back my toys."

He wondered if she'd get it, and when she did, he realized that though she was cynical she was also very smart.

"*Your* toys?" Her black eyebrows lifted in two beautiful, though skeptical, arches. "*You're* the crackpot inventor?"

Hunter started to defend himself but changed his mind. What good would it do? None.

"The last time I checked, I thought the toys belonged to the store, once they purchased them," Sylvie continued. "They're cute toys. Why don't you just rake in the money and enjoy?"

"It's not about money. Legally, they do belong to the store," he conceded, wondering how much she'd be willing to listen to him. So far, she'd listened more attentively than anyone else. "Morally, I'm responsible for them."

"Morally responsible for toys," she said slowly. "Those aren't evil little Chucky dolls, are they? They don't come to life and injure children, do they?"

She was so incredibly cynical, and yet there was just a tiny redeeming hint of humor. Or at least he thought there was. "The dolls, intrinsically, aren't evil. What was done to them—or what was done to *some* of them—is."

He had her attention.

"Done to them? As in someone hurt the dolls?"

He could see her backing away, wondering if he was crazy. "When I created the formula for the dolls, including the antibacterial material, herbs and vitamins, I thought I'd made a breakthrough discovery."

She was listening to him, but she was also sitting up. In a moment she would become afraid of him and stop listening. He had to make it fast. It was impossible, but this woman seemed to be the first person willing to consider his story.

"Everything was perfect, until I got a phone call a week ago. The caller threatened me—if I didn't pull the dolls, children would suffer. It wasn't clear if the person knew something about my formula, or if— Anyway, that's when I started trying to get my dolls back."

"And they were tested and found perfectly fine."

"*Two* dolls were tested," he said carefully. "Yesterday evening I got another call. Two children who'd received my dolls were deathly ill." Her eyes had gone china again, a clear blue that riveted him. "It may kill them. I'm certain the illness was caused by the dolls." He took a breath. "I had to get all of the dolls back, no matter how. I called KATZ Meow again, but they think I'm insane. They hung up on me."

"What about the police?" Sylvie asked.

"I tried. They laughed at me. I'm like the boy who cried wolf. They did the initial tests and found nothing. Now I'm viewed as either crazy or mean. I called judges, politicians, even the Center for Disease Control. I'm on the kook list. So I had to take matters into my own hands."

"Are all the dolls dangerous?" Sylvie asked.

He could have kissed her because she believed

enough to ask the question. "That's the terrible thing," he said. "I don't know what happened to them or how many were affected."

"Could it be something in the manufacturing process?" Sylvie sat up straighter, as if she were thinking more clearly.

"I don't know," he said, hearing the desperation in his own voice. "I can't prove anything. And since you already think I'm a nut case, you might as well hear the rest of it. I think someone broke into my plant and put something in my doll material. I think the dolls were deliberately poisoned!"

Chapter Two

Poisoned dolls! At Christmas! Egads, this sounds worse than something the evil Moriarty might conspire to do against Sherlock Holmes. Then again, as the good doctor-slash-Santa so aptly pointed out, he might be a nutcase. I can only trust that my little Christmas elf isn't susceptible to every good line that comes along, and judging from the sharp intelligence in her blue eyes, she's nobody's fool. And, not to be forgotten, I'm here to help her.

The first course of action is to get out of this van and see how the good doctor does with a needle and sutures. After years of watching Dr. Doolittle tend the wounds of his animal clientele, I know good stitching from bad. That's a nasty cut my sprite has on her head. I think I'll just tuck back into this sack of toys and make sure that he takes me wherever he takes her. That way, if he doesn't release her, I'll be able to take action.

SYLVIE LOOKED AT THE HAND extended to her. She almost reached out for it, and then the long lessons of her life kicked in. A proffered hand was often the prelude to a belt to the teeth.

"I can manage," she said haughtily.

"I'm sure you can. I was attempting to introduce myself. Hunter Semmes," he said.

The smile he wore was self-deprecating and held a large amount of charm. Sylvie instantly went on red alert. Doctors weren't usually the humble type. During her career as a clerk, she'd waited on thousands of them in stores. Mostly they were arrogant, pressed for time and certain that their money could buy everything that made life worth living. Hunter Semmes didn't strike her as a real doctor.

"What's your name?" he prompted.

"Puddin' and Tane."

His laugh was soft. "I won't ask again," he said, backing out of the van door and allowing her to find her own balance and crawl out. Her elf costume was short and low cut, and she realized that he had something of a view. It only made her hate Christmas more. Stupid, idiotic costume.

When she got out of the van she saw she was in a vast garage or warehouse. Boxes were stacked neatly at one end and labeled with Semmes Toy Shop, Thirty-fourth Street, New York, New York. At the sight of the address, she felt a chill run through her, but she was smart enough to keep her lip zipped. Once she got away, she'd be able to lead the cops back to him.

"If you feel weak, I'll be glad to assist you," he said. "Otherwise, I think you'd prefer to walk on your own."

"You get two points for astuteness," she said, finding her balance in the silly elf boots. She fell in step behind him. Even in the poorly fitting Santa costume, she could see that his shoulders were broad.

The rest of his physique was left to supposition since he was hauling the bag of dolls on his back.

Aware of where her thoughts had gone, she rolled her eyes. At thirty-four years of age, she wasn't the type to moon over a man. She'd learned the hard way that good looks didn't translate into good behavior. For the past three years she'd sworn off men altogether. Too much work for too little return.

She followed him up a short flight of stairs and waited while he unlocked a door. It made her nervous, but there seemed to be no other option. If she tried to turn and run, he'd catch her. Besides, he just didn't seem to be the desperado type. Not that she believed a word he'd said—but then again, there were the boxes of toys.

When he pushed open the door she stopped and caught her breath. The vast room was like a toy store. There were hundreds of animals, dolls and wooden toys on shelves and lying on worktables.

"Excuse the clutter," he said as he deposited the toy sack beside a work counter. "Just follow me."

She did, trying her best to look at everything and memorize the lay of the land. Just in case.

Hunter pressed a button, and a portion of the wall slid back to reveal an elevator door. Sylvie hesitated. Had the wall not moved, she'd never have known there was an elevator there. "What are you, some kind of Batman fan?"

Hunter's chuckle was slightly uncomfortable. "Not exactly."

"Right. Hidden doors, secret rooms. Where are we going?"

"My offices are on the second floor," he said.

"And I suppose you live in the penthouse."

He laughed again. "If you want to call the third floor a penthouse, then you can. Actually it's nothing quite so swank."

Swank! She hadn't heard that word in years, but it made her smile. He was an odd sort of man. He really wasn't the least bit arrogant. She got in the elevator and held her breath until the door opened, exposing a room so uncluttered and sparsely furnished that it was almost empty.

"I gave up my practice when I went into the toy business," he said. "I kept enough things on hand that I can take care of your head. In my better days, I was something of a good stitcher. With children, you get a lot of practice."

"You don't have to explain," she replied, aware that she wanted him to tell her more.

"This way." He opened a door and she stepped into a room with a large desk and an examining table. The only things on the desk were a daily planner—blank—and a framed photograph of a young boy: a dark-haired child with large brown eyes. A bit thin and sad looking.

Hunter walked to the desk and picked up the photograph. "My son," he said. "He died of leukemia. That's when I decided that I wasn't cut out to be a healer."

Sylvie prided herself on her tough guard, and she was unprepared for the surge of sympathy she felt for the stranger who stood before her. There was something in the way he held the photograph that smote her heart. Careful, she reminded herself instantly. This guy could be the Academy Award-winning nutcase of the century.

"I'm sorry," she said, making sure there was

enough frost in her voice not to let him know that she'd been moved.

"Yes, me, too." He replaced the picture and motioned to the table. "Have a seat, and I'll check that head."

"And then I'm free to go?"

"Free to go," he answered. "I intended to have the police chase me as a toy thief, not a kidnapper," he said. "The only thing I ask is that you contact the police and let them know that I didn't abduct you."

"But you did." Sylvie couldn't help but point this out.

"Legally, yes. Morally, no," he said, giving her that small grin again. "My intention wasn't to take you. If you hadn't fought like a wild thing, you'd be back at the store right this minute."

Sylvie felt her temper begin to rise. Wasn't it just like a man to put the blame on someone else? "Oh, certainly it was my fault. I'm the one who forced you to come into the store and take me hostage at gunpoint—"

"Water gunpoint," he corrected.

"I thought it was a real gun, and so did everyone else." At her words, his face drew into worried lines.

"I know. That concerns me," he said. "I didn't mean to frighten people so. It wasn't a very good plan, I'm afraid."

Dang him! Just when she had her righteous indignation worked up, he turned the tables by going all apologetic on her. "Well, just look at my head and let me out of here."

She almost regretted her words when he began to shuck out of the Santa costume. Beneath the red cloth he wore a plaid work shirt and jeans. And the broad shoulders gave way to a lean waist, narrow hips and long legs. For a medical man he was a very compelling package.

"Have a seat on the table," he said as soon as he was free of the costume.

Sylvie climbed reluctantly onto the table and immediately felt at a disadvantage. She waited while he washed his hands at a sink in the corner and then adjusted a light. She closed her eyes when his fingers gently touched her face and turned it so that he could see.

"It's not as bad as I thought," he said. He went to a cabinet and came back with a cotton ball soaked in antiseptic. The wet cotton ball was cold, but the antiseptic was hot as fire as he cleaned the wound.

She winced and he stopped.

"It's going to take a couple of stitches, but it should heal without a scar," he said. "Since it's just at the hairline, I don't think you'll be too disappointed."

She opened her eyes and found herself staring straight into his worried brown ones. "I'm not the kind of woman who gets all bent out of shape about a tiny cut. Just get on with it," she said because she felt a strange tumbling in her stomach that warned her of her own attraction to this man.

"You'd better lie back," he said, easing her down.

He turned away to prepare whatever he needed, and Sylvie closed her eyes. He would have been a good doctor with children. He clearly cared. She knew it by his touch. There had been precious little tenderness in her past, but she could recognize it.

"When did you quit practicing?" she heard herself ask. The sound of her own voice shocked her.

"After my son died, I lost the heart for it. That was about four years ago." Though he never looked away from his work, his hands faltered slightly. "You'd think that a man could protect his own child." He shifted to attend to the instruments that clanked as he laid them out.

"I'm not a doctor, but leukemia isn't something that comes from negligence," she said. She'd never considered herself kindhearted, but Hunter Semmes was so obviously suffering that she felt the need to say something to help.

"I should have been able to do something."

"Well, next time there's an election for God, I'll vote for you," she said, aware too late of the bitterness of her reply. "I'm sorry," she added. "I didn't mean that the way it sounded. It's just that sometimes there's nothing you can do." Oh, that was one she knew very well. "Where's your wife?" she asked, to cover the breach in her own defenses.

"After Brad died, she left."

Sylvie started to ask another question, then stopped. His past wasn't her business, and she'd stomped around in it quite enough.

He came back over, and she closed her eyes again and gritted her teeth as he deadened the wound and put in the stitches. He worked in silence but with a touch so sure and gentle that she felt herself relax.

"There you go," he said, brushing her hair back when he was finished. "Those stitches should come out in about a week."

His strong hands eased her up to a sitting position, and she found, once again, his intense brown gaze on her.

"Are you okay?"

She nodded. "Thanks."

"I am sorry. I don't know what I can do to make this up to you."

He looked so contrite. "Are you telling the truth about the toys?" she asked.

"I wish I weren't. I sold exclusively to KATZ Meow toy store in New York, so I have all of the toys back—except the ones that have already been bought. Somehow I'll have to find the people who bought them and get them back. My best hope is that they've been bought for Christmas presents. That'll give me," he thought a minute, "three days." He shook his head. "Only three days."

"I could help you." Sylvie amazed herself. "I could check the store computer and find out who bought the toys." She was even more amazed at the look of disbelief, followed by hope, on his face.

"You'd do that?"

What had she gotten herself into? "I suppose I could." She had just offered to do something illegal. But she wanted to do it. If children's lives were at stake...

"If we retrieve those toys, we might save some children. I'll go ahead with my plan and turn myself in to the authorities as the man who tried to rob the toy store. That way the publicity will get out, and if you contact the families who bought toys, they'll give them back willingly."

It was a great plan—except for the fact that it wouldn't work. "You can't," she said simply. "If you turn yourself in, they'll put you in a cell and forget about you until next spring. They'll think you're crazier than ever. And they'll tack a kidnapping charge on you no matter what I say. They might send you down to Bellevue for an evaluation, and by the time they're finished with you, Christmas will be over and the worst could have happened.''

''But—''

''I know what I'm talking about,'' Sylvie said. Growing up poor had enlightened her on the way the system worked in a big city. Hunter Semmes was a perfect candidate to be caught in the web. No one would care that he'd robbed a major store because he believed some toys were poisoned. If the officials got their hands on him, he'd end up in a mental ward or a cell.

''I know what I did was out of the ordinary, but I intended—''

''Intentions don't count for squat,'' she said, sliding off the table and to her feet. Now that she was feeling more like herself, she realized how tall he was. She had to look up to talk to him. ''You robbed a store and kidnapped an elf. Either you're a criminal or a nutcase. That's the way the law is going to see it.''

''Surely if I explain to them that I was trying to get publicity so I could warn people of the danger, they'll know that I didn't mean to do anything wrong.''

Sylvie felt exasperation begin to take hold. Hunter Semmes was an idealist. He was one of those people who actually thought it mattered what a person *meant* to do. He had a rough education in front of him.

''Think about this,'' she said, warming to her subject. ''Put aside your intentions. The result was that someone fired at you, into a crowd. And that resulted in me getting injured. Any number of other people could have been injured by a ricocheting bullet. The police aren't going to take kindly to a man who puts others at risk because he's acting out some harebrained scheme to save children."

She could see that she'd finally gotten to him. Light had dawned in his eyes.

"You're right," he said. "I knew it was a desperate plan, but I had no idea of the repercussions. More innocent people could have easily been hurt. I was a fool!"

Sylvie rolled her eyes. "Don't go too far, Doc. You were trying to do the right thing. Give yourself a little credit. If folks had listened to you, then you wouldn't have been in such a jam. Now, we just have to fix this ourselves, and it's obvious to me you need some help."

She was unprepared for the rush of warmth that spread through her when his eyes met hers. He reached out and touched her face. "You're going to help me?"

Sylvie closed her eyes and wondered why she'd suddenly become a good Samaritan, especially when she knew better. "I'll help," she said, opening her eyes. "I'm as big a fool as you are, but I'll help. Promise me one thing."

"What's that?" Hunter asked.

"Don't ever wear that Santa costume again. I hate Christmas."

Hunter's brown eyes went a dark, warm color. "I promise you that I won't wear that costume."

Sylvie stuck out her hand. "My name is Sylvie West. If you'll show me the door, I'll go back to the store and see what I can find out on the computer. And I'll tell everyone that I went to a doctor's office instead of coming here to your secret hideaway."

"Thanks," Hunter said, squeezing her hand.

HUNTER WATCHED WITH amusement as Sylvie hailed a cab and climbed in. The elf costume certainly wasn't suited for street wear. And her figure didn't help. She was tall and slender but wasn't lacking in the curve department. In fact, with her looks, she could easily have modeled. Somehow, though, he knew that that life wasn't one she would have chosen. She wasn't that kind of woman.

Two men walking down the street whistled at her, which prompted a very unladylike gesture on her part. He couldn't help but laugh. For a woman who looked like a lanky sprite, she had the mannerisms of a street urchin.

And he wondered if her early years hadn't been spent learning to survive on the streets.

He'd also noticed scars in her hairline. They weren't big. They were hardly noticeable, in fact. But somewhere along the line, Sylvie West had had a hard life. Perhaps on a playground, for she struck him as a person who went all-out at something, whether it was life or a game.

But he suspected that her scars had come from another source. What had she said—that she didn't get bent over a tiny cut? Well, she'd had a few in the past. The very idea of someone hurting her made his blood run hot.

For all of her toughness, there was a streak of kindness running straight through her. She'd learned to cover it up, but it was still there. How many other people would have offered to help a stranger who'd abducted her and almost gotten her shot?

He tidied his office, then went down to the workshop where he'd spent the past two years developing Molly McBright and Buster Bigboy. He looked around and felt a sense of failure. He'd worked so long and finally had begun to believe that he'd created something that would help children.

The bitter irony was that two youngsters were gravely ill, and that he might be the cause.

A pang of conscience tore into him. He'd told Sylvie the truth—almost all of it. What was eating at him was the possibility that he'd somehow messed up the formula for the dolls and created the toxic material himself.

He went to a table and picked up a Molly doll. Her blue eyes opened wide and her smile was as wistful as his wife's had been for the last six months of their marriage. He didn't blame Connie for leaving him. He'd been so sunk in despair and self-pity that he'd had nothing to give to her to help with her own grief. Now he saw the selfishness of his behavior, but it was too late. She'd gone on to find happiness somewhere else. And she was marrying Peyton Klepp, another doctor. Hunter wasn't surprised at the news—Peyton had a thriving practice and the reputation for living in the fast lane. He was a good-looking man and a skilled surgeon. A perfect match for Connie, and Hunter wished her only the best. They hadn't been able to hold on to their love for each other, but they had managed to remain friends. And at times, Hunter felt Connie, for all of her materialism, was the only person who really understood how deeply Brad's death had affected him.

The truth was, their son had been the glue that held their marriage together. When Brad died, everything else had come tumbling down.

Hunter went to his desk and picked up the photograph of Brad. He was staring at it when he felt something brush against his leg. Startled, he looked down to see a big black cat with golden eyes staring up at him.

"Meow," the cat said, rubbing vigorously against him.

"Where did you come from?" He bent down to scratch the cat.

"Meow-meow-meow!   Meow-meow-meow! Meow-meow-
meow-meow-meow!"

"'Jingle Bells'?" Hunter said with amazement. "You're singing "'Jingle Bells'?"

"Me-e-e-ow," the cat replied, nodding once.

Hunter shook his head. "An elf and a singing cat, all in one day. This is unbelievable."

Familiar did a figure eight through his legs, then lightly bit his shin.

Hunter picked the cat up in his arms. "Wherever you came from, you have a home here. For as long as you want. I only wish Brad could have heard you sing."

Familiar leaped lightly from Hunter's arms and landed on the desk. He went to the photograph and rubbed against the frame.

"So you think he heard you, do you?" Hunter asked. "Well, I believe that, too. So let's go up to the kitchen and make his favorite meal—hamburger steak. I haven't eaten all day."

He scooped the cat back into his arms and headed for the elevator.

HEAVEN, I'M IN HEAVEN. Hamburger steak isn't exactly the gourmet food I'm accustomed to eating, but it's

*one of my favorite staples. And who would have
thought I'd be so warmly adopted? Only problem is
that Eleanor and Peter will be looking for me. Good
thing I dumped my credit card in the toy sack. I'll
just have to remember to get it before I blow this
popsicle stand. Dr. Santa might accept a singing cat,
but he surely wouldn't believe in one with his own
platinum account. But then again, perhaps it's time
for Dr. Santa and the sprite to believe. A few miracles do seem to be in order this holiday season, and
I'm just the cat to deliver.*

*As for my rendition of "Jingle Bells," I know I
said a cat would never perform for a human, but he
was so sad. And he's in serious trouble. I couldn't
help myself. Maybe it's the Christmas spirit I'm feeling.*

*After a bit of hamburger steak and a nap, I'll have
to think about getting in touch with my humanoids
and then setting about helping the good doctor un-
knot this mess he's made.*

*Uh-oh, I hear sirens outside the window. I'm
afraid the fox has been run to ground. That hamburger steak is going to have to wait!*

HUNTER OPENED the warehouse doors when the police officers shoved a warrant against the glass panel.
He'd expected them, and he was as prepared for them
as he could be.

"Dr. Semmes, we're investigating an incident at a
toy store," Officer Welford said, eyes boring into
Hunter. "Where were you an hour ago?"

Hunter had anticipated being arrested. That had
been his goal, but now things had changed. As Sylvie

pointed out to him, he had to stay out of jail. "I was having a cup of coffee with my ex-wife."

"Is that so?" the officer said. "You weren't anywhere near KATZ Meow Toy Emporium?"

"I believe I've been ordered not to set foot on those premises," Hunter replied. "I'm not the kind of person who breaks the law just for the fun of it." He was walking a thin line and he knew it.

The cop stared at him. "No, you're the kind of person who might do something crazy, like steal a shelfful of toys."

"I'm a toy maker. Why would I want to steal toys?" Hunter countered.

"Because the only toys stolen were those you invented."

Hunter arched his eyebrows. "Someone stole my dolls? All of them?"

"We want to have a look around."

Hunter stepped back, ushering the two officers inside. Sylvie had accused him of having a Batman complex, and it wasn't the first time he'd heard such an accusation. One good thing about his childish fantasies—the van was perfectly hidden behind a false wall. And his living quarters were inaccessible, except via the secret elevator. He'd enjoyed designing his workshop and living space. It had been for fun, but now it was coming in handy. So he had a little bit of a Bruce Wayne complex. So what? Batman was one of the good guys.

The officers checked the entire ground floor. They went through the toy shop, but the stolen dolls were as carefully concealed as the van. The policemen checked the second and third floors, unaware of the space he'd carved out for his office or apartment. To them it was all one big toy factory.

"Okay," the cops said. "You got an address and phone number for your ex-wife? We'll want to talk to her."

Hunter gave them the information. As soon as they were gone, he picked up the phone and placed the call to Connie.

"The cops are going to ask if I was with you today, about two hours ago. We had coffee at the Java Break, okay?"

"Hunter? What's wrong?"

"Will you do this for me?" he asked.

"Hunter, this sounds a little crazy," she said softly. "What's going on?"

"It's about the dolls. Someone robbed KATZ Meow. A clerk—Sylvie West—was kidnapped. Briefly, I need an alibi."

There was a long silence on the other end of the phone.

"Hunter, you need to talk to someone. A professional. Since Brad died, you've been getting stranger and stranger. I worry—"

"Connie, the police are going to call. Either you're willing to tell them we were having coffee or not. Which is it?" He had no one else he could ask. He'd let his professional relationships fall away—and his friends. Connie had a point, when she argued that his life was out of balance. He'd spent the past four years alone, developing toys.

"I will. On one condition. That you promise me you'll talk to someone. This obsession with toys is…well, it isn't healthy."

"Okay," he agreed. "Just cover for me."

"You didn't do it? You didn't rob that store, did you? You know if I get involved in something illegal, Peyton will be furious with me. He's high profile, and about to be named chief of staff. Bad publicity—"

"Don't be ridiculous," Hunter said evenly. "I'll check back with you. And thanks, Connie."

Chapter Three

Stuck in traffic that spurted forward and then slammed to a halt to stall for fifteen minutes, Sylvie rubbed her neck and sought patience as she heard the sirens headed toward Hunter's toy shop.

She considered going back, then decided that the best thing she could do would be to check in at the store, and make it clear she hadn't been kidnapped. If Hunter was arrested, she'd figure a way to bond him out.

As long as he kept his mouth shut.

If he went on and on about poisoned toys, they'd send him for a mental evaluation, and by the time he got out of the clutches of the doctors, it would be too late. Her anxiety level peaked as she thought about that.

She turned and was staring out the back window of the cab with such intensity that the cabby spoke to her.

"You want to go back or what?" he asked.

"If I want to go back, I'll tell you," she answered sharply.

"Hey, I was trying to be of assistance."

"I'm sorry," Sylvie said, and meant it. She'd gotten so used to snapping at people that she'd gone off half-cocked.

"Where do you work?" the man asked.

Sylvie had forgotten about her costume. She looked down and felt a rueful smile cross her face. "KATZ Meow. I'm a Christmas elf."

"I was gonna take my kids in there tomorrow."

"They'll love it," Sylvie replied, and was surprised to realize that she knew they would. Kids did love the toy store. Especially at Christmas.

The cab pulled to the street in front of the store, and she jumped out and thrust money at the driver.

"No charge," the driver said. "Put a smile on a kid's face for me."

Astounded, Sylvie still held out the money as he drove away. She turned to walk into the store and was swarmed by staff members who were so relieved to see her that she was genuinely touched. She'd never thought that any of her co-workers would really care if anything happened to her.

"I'm okay," she insisted.

"Tell us what happened," Alice, one of her co-workers, insisted as she rubbed Sylvie's arms as if to warm her up. "You poor child, did he hit you on the head?"

"No, he didn't hit me. He took me to a doctor and let me go," she said, touched by the worry on Alice's kind face. She was the one co-worker who'd tried to mother Sylvie with delicious homemade treats. "I'm okay, just a little flustered."

"You're going to press charges, aren't you?" Alice asked.

Sylvie thought a moment. "No. I'm not hurt. I'd prefer to just forget the whole thing."

"I don't think that's an option," Alice said, pointing at two policemen who were walking rapidly in her direction.

"I feel a little faint," Sylvie said, leaning against Alice's strong shoulder. "Maybe I should go home and talk to the police later."

Before anyone could object, Sylvie slipped through the crowd and headed into the store. The place was a maze and she could easily lose the cops. All she had to do was keep moving.

Dang it! She didn't want to talk to the police, because that would entail lying. Growing up in a rough part of town, she'd had a few brushes with the law, but she'd never lied. The policemen would want to know if she could identify the man who'd abducted her in a lineup. They might even ask for the name of the doctor who'd treated her injury. Those were questions she didn't want to answer.

She made a swing by the checkout counter in the department where she worked, proclaimed her good health and exhaustion, grabbed her coat and purse, and scurried on, just ahead of the officers of the law. She made it to the employee exit and fled into the fading afternoon. Unwilling to wait for a city bus, she set out walking. It would be easy to mingle with the rush of humanity on the street and get lost. Her elf costume was covered by her winter coat, and though her elf boots were a little goofy, they weren't totally outrageous for New York.

Though she hadn't intended it, she found herself headed in the general direction of Hunter's building. She was worried about him. She'd heard the sirens. What if he was in jail?

She attempted to harden her feelings. This was ridiculous. The past had taught her that caring for others, particularly strangers, could only lead to trouble. She had to keep focused on the fact that no matter what Hunter Semmes said, he was a criminal. He'd kidnapped her and nearly gotten her killed.

But as she paced along the city street, she argued with herself. His intentions had been to save children.

Or so he said, the other side of her interjected.

But then she remembered his touch as he'd taken care of her head. Her hand reached up and brushed the bandage. Hunter Semmes might be crazy, but he wasn't a kidnapper.

She stopped at a phone booth and made a call to the precinct house that would handle the district where the toy store was located. When she asked if a Hunter Semmes was on the jail docket, she was relieved to get a negative. She hung up and found herself smiling at a young mother with two tow-headed kids.

"Merry Christmas," the woman said, smiling back.

"Merry Christmas to you," Sylvie said, surprised at the sense of joy that came from a strange woman's smile.

"Merry Christmas," the two children yelled, laughing.

Sylvie walked away with the most peculiar feeling. She hated Christmas. It was all so commercial and fake and consumer oriented. So why was she smiling?

She caught a glimpse of her reflection in the window of a gift shop. Even as she stared at her silly grin, the window lights burst into life, and the Christmas tree, decorated with handmade bows and ornaments, lit up. It was as if her own soul filled with some of the gentle light, and she hardly recognized the expectant face of the dark-haired young woman who stared back at her.

She had a mental image of herself as a young girl, staring into shop windows at Christmas. Even when she was old enough to know better, she'd always hoped that Santa would find her and her brothers and sisters. She'd always thought that this year, since they'd all been good, the Christmas miracle would happen and they would have a toy or a pretty dress or something left for them by the man in the red suit.

It was normally a memory so painful that it made her angry, but this time she recognized the power in it—the ability of a child to hope, to believe in goodness.

She was about to turn away from the window when she noticed the man's reflection. He stood behind her, several feet back, a nondescript man dressed in an ordinary brown overcoat and a hat. But she'd seen him earlier in the day, at KATZ Meow. And again at the corner several blocks back. When she'd stopped to read a poster, she'd seen him looking at her.

She turned around suddenly, hoping to confront him. But even as she moved, he darted forward, rushing her. Before she could step out of his way she felt his arms closing around her. A car skidded to the curb, and the back door swung open.

The man who held her was trying to bundle her toward the car.

"Help!" she screamed. "Help me!"

Several people stopped and stared, but no one

came forward to help her as the man pulled her, inch by inch, toward the car.

"Help!" she screamed again.

"This is New York. No one's going to help you, so shut up," the man whispered tersely as he tried to push her into the back seat.

Sylvie braced her legs on the side of the car, bent her knees and then straightened with all of her strength. The man toppled backward, and she fell to the gutter.

Before she could get to her feet, a plump, elderly gentleman came out of the crowd. He wielded a golf umbrella as if it were a rapier, and with several hard jabs and a few slashing blows, he drove her attacker away from her. The man jumped into the back of the car, and it squealed away.

Sylvie, assisted by the elderly man, got slowly to her feet.

"Thanks," she said, glaring at the rest of the on-lookers who slunk away now that the action was over. "He was trying to kidnap me."

"Don't tell me! You're a wealthy heiress," the man said. "Your abductor was going to ask for ransom." His blue eyes twinkled. "Are you a Vander-bilt or a Carnegie?"

Sylvie didn't find the situation funny—after all, it was her second kidnap attempt of the day. But she did find the old gentleman charming. "Sorry to burst your bubble, but I'm nobody. They certainly weren't after me for ransom. There's not a person in the world who'd pay a dime for me."

The old man laughed and dusted at a soiled spot on her coat. "You exaggerate," he said. "But if it wasn't ransom, why were they after you?"

There was keen intelligence in his bright blue eyes. She looked in the direction the car had gone. It had been a plain black car. Big, with four doors. She hadn't had the time or the presence of mind to get the license plate or even the make of it. "I don't have a clue," she answered.

She heard how jerky her words were, and it was only then that she realized she was shaking. Delayed reaction, she thought. She'd very nearly been taken hostage, and this second kidnapper had shown none of Hunter Semmes's gentleness.

"You don't owe money to the mob, do you?" the man asked.

Sylvie started to snap out a reply, but when she turned to the old man, his eyes had almost disappeared in the laugh lines around them.

"I don't owe money to anyone," Sylvie said. And she didn't want to discuss it anymore. It dawned on her that two kidnappings in one day couldn't possibly be coincidence. This abduction attempt was related to her earlier escapade with Hunter Semmes. And if it wasn't Hunter, then it had to be the opposition—the people who might be trying to poison children! The idea of it made her stomach knot with such force that her knees almost buckled.

"Why don't we step inside this little tavern and have something to drink," the man suggested.

Surprised, Sylvie looked at him—hard. He wasn't coming on to her, he was simply being nice. She looked up and down the street. Perhaps it would be a good idea to have a drink with the old gentleman. The possibility of her would-be attacker knowing where she lived—following her home—was frightening.

"My name is Chester Fenton," the man said, offering the crook of his arm to her. "I think we could both use a cup of Irish coffee, and this place happens to make the best in town," he said.

Sylvie took his arm, surprised to find it so strong and muscular. His hair was silvery in the dim twilight, and she'd assumed he was in his seventies. But it was hard to tell these days. She walked beside him into Lou's Tavern and took the seat he held for her.

"Two coffees, Irish," Chester said as he settled across the small table from her. "Now, Miss…"

"Sylvie West," she supplied.

"Sylvie West. What's going on here?"

"I wish I knew. For certain," she said. "I wish I knew," she repeated. To her amazement, she felt tears burning in her eyes and her throat begin to close. She hadn't cried in ten years! Not even at a movie. What was happening to her emotions? She'd been smiling at people, and now she was about to burst into tears in front of a perfect stranger.

She looked up to find Chester holding out a clean, white handkerchief to her.

"Take it, my dear," he said. "Honest emotion is nothing to be ashamed of. You've had a bad scare. A cry will do you a world of good."

Sylvie felt the first tear coast down her cheek. "He frightened me," she said by way of explanation, further amazed that she was admitting to a stranger that anything had frightened her. Showing weakness, she'd learned early on, was an invitation to brutality.

Since she hadn't taken the handkerchief, he reached across the table and gently brushed the tear away. "Anyone would have been frightened," he said reasonably. "But you're safe now. And together, we're going to figure out why he tried to grab you. If you aren't an heiress, perhaps you're famous. Do you sing?"

The old gentleman's light humor was the perfect balm. Sylvie felt her tears recede, and a smile lit up her face. "If anyone heard me sing, they'd be trying to give me away, not snatch me," she said.

"I'm a bit of a blue yodeler myself," he said, nodding wisely. "But my wife, before she passed away, used to ask me sing. She knew how much I loved it, and she pretended that she enjoyed listening to me."

Sylvie wasn't certain, but she thought she saw a tear in the old man's eye. She didn't consider herself a perceptive person, especially not when it came to the emotional needs of others. She'd tried very hard not to be. She had constructed armor against all the pain and suffering in the world. But the old gentleman across the table had penetrated her defenses. "I can't imagine someone loving me enough to pretend that I could sing," she said. "That must have been wonderful."

"Indeed it was," he answered. "Love is the best gift to give. Or receive."

The waitress brought the coffees, and Sylvie sipped the delicious concoction. The warmth of the coffee and the faint bracing taste of the liquor made her feel better. "How long has your wife been dead?" she asked.

"Five years. They say when you get older, time passes faster. Until Maria died, time did fly. Now, though, it sometimes seems the days are endless. Especially at Christmas. Maria loved this season. She baked and decorated and wrapped presents. She was a joy to watch.''

Sylvie felt as if all of her troubles were suddenly reduced to mere warts in the light of this man's loss. It was tragic never to have been loved. But to have found the one person who loved you completely and totally—and then to have death step in and steal that person—that must be the worst.

''You know, tomorrow I'm going to St. Mary's Orphanage to take a few presents to the children there. Why don't you come with me?'' he asked.

Her first inclination was to refuse, but something made her reconsider. The orphanage wasn't a place she wanted to be at Christmas, but she couldn't deny the old gentleman her company. ''I have to work, but maybe we could go during lunch.''

''Will you wear your elf costume?'' he asked, beaming.

''Certainly,'' she agreed, glad to understand the part she was expected to play.

''Maria used to be my elf,'' he said. ''I can't help but think she'd be delighted with you in that role. You resemble her greatly you know, when she was a young woman.''

''Is that why you helped me?'' Sylvie asked.

''It was what made me look your way before the trouble started, but I suppose I would have tried to help anyone.'' He reached across the table and patted her hand. ''Finish your coffee, my dear. I have to get home and make sure my presents for tomorrow are all wrapped and ready to go.''

Sylvie drained her cup and allowed Chester Fenton to help her with her coat.

"May I escort you home?" he asked.

She shook her head. "Tend to your presents. Where shall I meet you tomorrow?"

"At St. Mary's, at noon," he said.

"I know right where it is," Sylvie said, but that was as far as she went. She had no intention of telling him that she'd spent four years in the orphanage. Her time there hadn't been unpleasant, merely unnoticed. It would be good to go back and bring some joy to the children there.

HUNTER CLOSED THE DOOR behind the police officers, relieved that their questions had been cursory. His medical title was a safe shield—few people would truly suspect a pediatrician of trying to rob a toy store.

He'd been lucky, too.

Along with making toys, he also had a fascination with mechanical devices. Before Connie had left him, she'd become annoyed with his inventions and tinkering. He sighed at the memory. He wanted to be a man who helped others, someone who brought goodness to those around him. But look where that had led him. There was every possibility his grand dreams had ended up poisoning children.

He went into his toy shop and looked around. The idea of punishment by the law didn't scare him. The thought of innocent children suffering because of something he'd created terrified him. There was no legal punishment that would compare to the nightmare of that.

Moving to his files, he pulled out the folder that contained the formulas he'd developed to create Molly McBright and Buster Bigboy. His formula was encrypted, and he felt a flash of bitter amusement. He'd known that the toy industry was highly competitive.

The money to be made in creating the next Cabbage Patch Doll or Barney sensation was incredible. And where there was money, there was always greed. But Hunter didn't care about the money. In developing Molly and Buster, he'd hoped to introduce toys that brought pleasure as well as good health.

Sure, money would be nice. There was never enough of it. At least there hadn't been for Connie. She'd gotten angry when he'd given up his Park Avenue practice. It didn't matter that he was home more, available to care for Brad.

He slapped the folder on the desk, stood up and began to pace. Why did he keep going over and over the same ground? It was past. Over. Done. *Fini.*

Connie was about to be remarried, and was happy from all indications. Brad was dead. The hard truth was that even if Brad had not contracted leukemia, he and Connie would have divorced. They had grown apart. Perhaps they'd always been different, and he hadn't seen it. It didn't matter. She was getting on with her life, and when they did talk, she sounded happy. He was glad for her, even if it made him wonder if all of the problems of their marriage had been with him.

Maybe he *was* a kid in a grown man's body. Maybe it was ridiculous to want to do something wonderful, something that would benefit mankind. Maybe it was stupid to think that he could do it by inventing a toy.

He returned to the worktable, picked up his folder and replaced it in the file. No matter how many times he went over the formula, he couldn't find a reason why anything in his dolls should make a child sick. And if it wasn't in his formula, then he had to find the person who'd added it. There was no time for self-pity if a criminal was on the loose.

He took the elevator up to his third-floor living quarters. As he pushed open the door, he heard something break in the kitchen. His hand froze on the doorknob. No one was supposed to be in his place. He listened intently and heard the soft snick of a door. Someone was there. Someone was in his kitchen.

He eased to the closet and slipped his hand around Brad's old baseball bat. Then slowly, quietly, he started toward the kitchen.

Chapter Four

Thank goodness Dr. Semmes isn't one of those health-nut doctors. Check out his larder. Yumm! Smoked salmon with a side serving of brie. This is heaven, and far superior to the hamburger steak the good doctor mentioned. And whipping cream. Yes, indeedy, this isn't going to be hard duty at all. I'll just have a little snack and then mosey around the toy shop again.

You'd think that a humanoid who eats like this would be pudgy, but not our mysterious toy maker. He's tall, lean and kind. As my old grannycat used to say, "Handsome is as handsome does," and Doc seems to qualify in both departments. All in all he seems to be a guy who bought into old-fashioned values. Interesting. I've made an extensive tour of his place. A lot can be learned by an observant puss. Take, for instance, the list of city orphanages I found, all marked and checked with different toys. A few were Mollys and Busters, but many were toys the good doctor purchased and arranged to have delivered. He isn't simply trying to drum up publicity for his own dolls—in fact, he's an anonymous donor.

I watched the interaction between my little sprite

and the doctor. Humanoids have more layers of self-defense than an onion has skins. I mean, both Clotilde and I had hard lives before we adopted our human families. That didn't stop us from doing a little midnight yowling. We met, accepted the attraction, and got busy with the courtship. If I don't give these two a big push, they'll wall each other off in an effort to keep from getting hurt. Criminy! I can't for the life of me figure out how enough humanoids managed to get together to become the dominant species. That's a mystery not even Familiar can solve.

But enough philosophizing, it's time to eat. Oops! That dish was a little slippery. Oh! No! Crash and burn! Crash and burn! I hope the good doctor has a maid. I hate cleaning up a mess. Then again, cats aren't expected to clean things up. We're famous for our ability to wreck a place. I suppose I could just play dumb and see if he'll tend to the wreckage. But I can salvage that big ole hunk of salmon. I didn't want the onions and mushrooms, anyway, though they were quite well prepared. I wonder if he has a cook. This could prove to be a very interesting assignment.

But do I detect the pitter-patter of big feet? Someone is trying very hard to creep into the kitchen. I think I'm caught red-handed.

HUNTER HEFTED the baseball bat and was ready to swing when he saw the broken dish on the floor. The refrigerator door was wide open, and in the light spilling out into the dark kitchen, he saw the black cat. The feline looked up at him, meowed and then returned to nibbling at the salmon.

For a long moment Hunter looked at the cat and refrigerator. Had the cat actually opened the door and knocked the food out? There could be no other explanation. So the feline had decided not to wait for him to cook. He was an impatient rascal.

"How did you get up here?" Hunter asked, realizing he'd last seen the cat on a lower level. He didn't remember it on the elevator. Then again, the cat had gotten into his toy shop without being detected. It was, apparently, a pretty smart cat. "So, do you like the salmon?" Hunter asked, bending down to pick up the broken dish. "Perhaps you'd like it served on china?"

"Meow." The cat rubbed against his leg.

"Is that a yes?" he asked, laughing at himself. He had the craziest idea that the cat understood what he was asking.

"Meow." The cat jumped up on the counter and then batted the cabinet door where the dishes were kept.

"Well, I'll be," Hunter said, getting a saucer and putting the remainder of the salmon on it. "I guess it's a good thing I'm not hungry."

The cat didn't respond, but instead tore into the fish.

Hunter stroked the cat's gleaming black coat. "I don't know where you came from, but someone took excellent care of you. They're going to be very worried."

The cat looked up at him, golden eyes glowing in the semidark kitchen. He'd polished off the fish, and he yawned and stretched, then walked into the foyer and over to the elevator.

"Meow."

Hunter hesitated.

"Meow."

"I can't believe you want me to get the elevator." And then he recalled that on the first and second floors, there were small tables beside the panel of elevator buttons. The cat had been able—he stopped himself. Cats didn't punch elevator buttons. Not even refrigerator-opening, salmon-stealing cats.

"Me-ow!"

It was a command if he'd ever heard one. He pressed the button to open the door. "First or second floor?" he asked, amazed that he was considering such a flight of fancy.

"Meow."

"I take it that means first." He got on with the cat. It occurred to him that the animal was ready to leave. He'd eaten, explored, and now that night had fallen, perhaps he was eager to go home. But on the first floor, the cat exited the elevator and went straight into the workshop. Without a single hesitation, the cat went to the place where he'd hidden the sack of dolls. Clawing at the door, he once again began to cry.

Hunter brought out the sack, and the cat instantly disappeared inside it. In a moment he came out with something in his mouth.

Taking the item from the cat, Hunter recognized it as a credit card. Platinum. And attached to a breakaway kitty collar. When he looked closer, he saw the name on the card. Familiar Detective Agency. Beside the name was a black-cat logo.

"I don't believe this," he said, taking the card to a telephone on the worktable. He called information, and in a matter of moments had a telephone number in Washington, D.C. He dialed, wondering what he would actually say when someone answered—'Hello, I have your cat'?

The phone rang three times before an answering device was activated and a woman's sleek, elegant voice spoke to him. "This is the Familiar Detective Agency. Familiar is in New York at the moment, but he'll be back January third. His rates are reasonable and there hasn't been a case he hasn't solved. He is the only mystery-solving cat available for private cases. Leave a name and number and one of his human employees will return your call."

Almost too astounded to speak, Hunter fumbled out a message that he had the cat and would like someone to call him back. When he looked around to see where Familiar had gone, he found him nosing at the packages of dolls. He was sniffing them like a dog.

"Watch out, Familiar," Hunter said, pushing the package away. "I'm not certain what's in there. If it makes children sick, it might not be good for a cat. Not even one who thinks he's a detective."

Familiar looked up at him and nodded. Then he hopped to the counter and pawed the remote control, turning on the television that was set high on a shelf. The screen flashed to life.

Hunter instantly recognized the New York Children's Hospital and the network newscaster who stood outside it, talking into a microphone.

"It's too early to call this an epidemic, but it would appear that some type of serial poisoner is on the loose here in New York City. Authorities won't confirm the source of the poison—in fact we feel they don't know. But two more children have been hospitalized and are in grave condition. That makes a total of four children. Mayor Juliano has declared an all-out war on the villain who is doing this, and police are on the alert. In the meantime, parents should watch their children closely. No candy from strangers, no unusual foods or snacks.''

The news anchor came on the screen. ''Tell us, Kip, how will this impact the holiday economy?''

The scene went back to the reporter at the hospital. ''Well, Peter, it's bad news for retailers. Since the scare started two days ago with the first two sick children, candy sales are down fifty percent. And that's just the tip of the iceberg. The panic is expected to make food sales plummet. Restaurants, which usually enjoy a rush of business from shoppers, will also be hit hard. Economically, this Serial Santa, as the poisoner is being called, is hitting New York City pretty hard.''

The news anchor came back on screen. ''We'll keep you updated on events as they happen. Kip will remain at the hospital for updates on the condition of the two latest victims of the Serial Santa.''

Hunter snapped off the television, his heart pounding. Another two children. He picked up the phone and dialed the hospital. In a moment he had the nurses' desk on the pediatric floor, and he was waiting for Lila Vernon, one of his favorite nurses from the days when he'd still practiced.

''Dr. Semmes,'' she said, delight clear in her voice. ''How are you?''

''Fine.'' He tried not to sound panicky. ''Those two kids they brought in, would you mind giving me their names?''

''It's against hospital policy,'' she reminded him.

"I'm a doctor," he countered.

"No longer practicing—and it's a shame. We miss you, Hunter. Will you come back?"

He hadn't thought of practicing in a long time, and he was surprised to find that he didn't miss it. Well, he didn't miss it as much as he'd thought he would. What he missed were the cases where the child got better and went home strong and healthy. He didn't miss at all the cases that ended differently.

"Not this week," he answered, keeping it light.

"I've got the patient list. The two little girls are Ellie and Nellie Wescott. Twins."

Hunter felt his heart sink. Two little girls were sick because of a doll he'd created. In all likelihood, they would spend Christmas in the hospital. "How bad are they?" he asked.

"They're sick," Lila said. "But they're holding their own."

Hunter recognized an opportunity when he saw one. "Have you got a toxicology report?" If he had a clue what to hunt for, he could begin to examine the dolls and figure how the substance had gotten into them.

"It's odd, Dr. Semmes. They display symptoms of poisoning, but we've run tests for arsenic, strychnine, lead, all the household chemicals. Nothing shows up. We're culturing bacteria—nothing there yet. The parents have gone through extensive interviews. The children didn't sample any strange foods anywhere."

"You're certain of that?" Hunter knew the answer but he had to ask.

"They're only two years old. These parents keep close tabs on them. And those other two cases. Those kids live across town so it wouldn't seem to be an environmental factor. It's a real mystery.''

Except Hunter knew the common denominator. His dolls. The only good thing was that he'd recovered almost all of the rest of his stock. Or he hoped he had. His fingers clutched the phone. He hadn't heard from Sylvie West, and she was supposed to check the computer list at the store to make sure no dolls had been sold. What if there were other children with Molly or Buster? He felt a surge of true panic.

''If you hear anything on those children, will you let me know?''

''Sure, but what's your interest?'' the nurse asked.

''Personal. I've been considering going into research. This case fascinates me.''

''Tired of making toys?'' Lila Vernon asked. ''We'd love to see you back here. There's not a day goes by that someone doesn't mention your name. You know you could come back in research. You wouldn't have to see patients. Perhaps you could even solve the mystery of what's happening to these children. It's pitiful to see them so sick.''

''I have some ideas in that area,'' he said carefully. ''I'll let you know if we find anything definitive.''

''Thanks, Lila.'' He hung up the phone, all too aware that the demons of anxiety had a firm hold on him. He checked the time—nearly nine. His thoughts wandered to the woman who'd offered to help him. Chances were she just wanted to make an escape and was perfectly willing to do or say whatever it took to get away from him. He was foolish to count on help from her.

Still, he couldn't help but feel let down. She'd looked as if she believed him. And if she didn't, nobody would. She'd seen his place, he'd told her about personal things, private pain that he'd never told anyone.

What was it about Sylvie West that had made him open up? Her china-blue eyes were clear in his memory—the sharp intelligence, the guardedness. He knew instantly that her very guardedness had made him want to open to her. The scars in her hairline showed she'd seen more than her share of harsh treatment. He shook his head twice. He was always a sucker for someone who'd been hurt. That was why he'd trained to be a doctor.

Familiar rubbed against his leg, and he bent down to pull him into his lap. He'd never thought to get a pet. They didn't live long enough, not even with the best care—they died too soon. And his heart couldn't take another loss.

"Shakespeare was wrong," he whispered into Familiar's black fur. "'Tis *not* better to have loved and lost than never to have loved at all. 'Tis far better to protect your heart and never suffer."

The black cat reached up and put a paw on his lips. "Meow." He shook his head.

Hunter didn't doubt what the cat was saying. "I can't take more heartbreak."

Familiar moved his paw from Hunter's lips down to his chest, right over his heart. He tapped lightly there.

"You're saying my ticker's in pretty good shape." Hunter found that the cat had greatly cheered him. It was true. His son's death had almost killed him. But it hadn't. He was still alive, and at thirty-six he had more than a few good years left. Years he would spend alone if he didn't let someone into his life.

''Meow,'' the cat said, golden eyes intensely staring into his.

''I don't know where you came from,'' Hunter said, stroking the cat's back, ''but I have to believe that you showed up in my life as a messenger. And I'm going to try to pay attention.''

Before he finished the sentence the phone rang. His heart raced ahead with the hope that it was Sylvie West. And when he heard her voice, he gave the cat one big grin.

''The store closes at eleven, and then the staff will be gone by midnight. I have a key to the employee door, so we can go in then and try to open the computer,'' Sylvie said, whispering swiftly.

''Are you okay?'' Hunter asked, his first concern for her. She sounded afraid.

''Someone tried to abduct me off the street. A man in a black car.'' Her words rushed out like a torrent of water. ''I'm afraid.''

She was afraid, and yet she was still willing to help him. Hunter was well aware of the miracle of such a thing. And it was the first real evidence he had that there was someone working against him. ''Did he hurt you?''

''No, he just scared me. An elderly gentleman beat him off with his umbrella.''

Hunter could picture the scene, and it left him worried and angry. ''But the attacker didn't hurt you?''

''No,'' and her voice calmed. ''I'm really okay.''

''Did he say anything? Did he do anything that might give you a hint who he is or what he wanted?''

There was a pause. ''No. He followed me from the store. Unless it was because of what happened with you, I don't know why he'd go after me.''

"I think you're right about that. Where are you now?"

"In a restaurant. I didn't want to go home."

She didn't have to say that she was afraid someone would be waiting for her. "Give me the address. I'll come get you. You can stay at my place tonight."

There was another hesitation. "Okay," she said, relief clear in her voice as she gave the address.

"Just wait there," Hunter said. "Promise me you won't leave for any reason."

"I promise."

They hung up, and Hunter grabbed his coat. As he started out the door to the garage, he realized the cat was right at his side. He almost put the cat back in his apartment, but he didn't. "So Mr. Familiar, cat detective, I have a case for you."

"Meow," Familiar answered, slapping at the panel that hid the van.

SYLVIE REPLACED THE telephone and turned back to the restaurant. Her breath caught in her throat when she saw the man in the overcoat standing in a line to be seated. He wasn't looking at her, and she had a rush of hope that his presence was coincidental.

That hope was dashed when he slowly turned his head, met her eye-to-eye and smiled.

Her first impulse was to rush out into the night, but she stopped herself. In the neighborhood where she'd grown up, the tough, older boys often played games where they would flush a weaker child out into the open. Then they would surround him and take what they wanted or merely give him a beating. She'd learned the value of hanging tight behind protective cover. She'd also learned the value of bravado.

Straightening her back, she walked straight across the restaurant to the man. She could see the shock on his face as he watched her dead-on approach.

Before she was halfway across the restaurant, he turned and left. Her smile of satisfaction was short-lived as she realized he could as easily lurk in the shadows and jump out at her and Hunter. He was more dangerous in the dark. Her ploy had been brave but foolhardy.

She returned to her table and found that the waiter had delivered her garden salad and water. While she nibbled at the salad, she watched the black-clad waiters swirl around her, delivering steaming platters of food. Her mouth watered and her stomach growled. But her paycheck was already spoken for, and dining in an expensive restaurant wasn't part of her agenda.

"More water?" a waiter asked with raised eyebrows.

"Please," Sylvie answered. "And another slice of lemon," she added for good measure.

At last she looked up to see Hunter crossing to her table. Her heart gave an erratic thump, and she felt blood rush to her face. He was a handsome man. Her body's reaction to him upset her. She'd learned her lesson about attractive men, hadn't she?

"Sylvie, are you sure you're okay?" he asked, coming to kneel beside her in a gesture that made several people look their way.

Hunter was oblivious to the people around him, his attention focused on Sylvie—and that made her heart beat even faster. He seemed to really care.

"I'm okay." She looked at the tablecloth where

cracker crumbs had clustered. The empty plastic wrappers testified to the entire basket of crackers she'd eaten, and she felt embarrassed.

He followed her gaze. "And hungry, too. And you waited for me." He took the seat across from her. "They have excellent seafood here. Shall I order for both of us?"

Sylvie was taken aback. She hadn't expected to eat, and now she wasn't sure what to say. She couldn't afford a meal in this restaurant.

"The grilled tuna is truly superb, if you like seafood."

"That sounds wonderful," she said, deciding to live dangerously.

Hunter signaled the waiter, who arrived with a far different attitude. He took Hunter's order, including wine and dessert, with an approving smile. "We might as well enjoy the food," Hunter said as he sat back in his chair, "we've got a couple of hours to kill before we can get into the store."

Sylvie started to answer and felt something at her ankles. Something warm and furry. She started to look under the tablecloth but Hunter reached across and touched her arm. "Don't," he whispered, a conspiratorial glint in his dark eyes. "It's the cat. He wanted to come."

Sylvie felt her eyes widen. "In the restaurant?"

"That's why I ordered the tuna. He seems to be a real connoisseur of seafood."

She leaned closer to Hunter, catching the scent of aftershave that was sharp and clean. Like Hunter. It was as if every detail of him struck her anew. "It's against the health code to have an animal in a restaurant," she said.

"I know," he answered. "Familiar isn't just an animal. He's a detective."

Sylvie lifted one eyebrow. Coming from anyone else, she might have thought he'd gone completely round the bend. But from Hunter, it didn't seem unreasonable. "How do you know this?" she asked.

"It's a long story," Hunter said, buttering the fresh bread the waiter delivered and offering a bite under the table. "Let's just say that as far-out as it sounds, this is one thing I can prove."

Warmth seemed to gently wash over Sylvie. Hunter had a sparkle in his eyes, and he was looking at her as if she were something of great worth. She wasn't surprised when he reached across the linen cloth and touched her hand. "Thank you, Sylvie. You've chosen to help me, at great risk to yourself, when no one else would. It's a rare gift."

She'd only recently talked with another man about gifts, and she remembered Chester Fenton's words clearly. He'd spoken of the gift of love. She was about to tell Hunter about the old gentleman when she looked up.

Outside the window stood the overcoat man. He lifted up one of Hunter's dolls—a Molly McBright. In one brutal gesture he popped the head off the doll.

Chapter Five

Hunter saw the horror on Sylvie's face, but by the time he turned around, the window was empty.

"Who was it?" he asked.

"The man who tried to abduct me. He had a doll." She closed her eyes, and Hunter saw the effort she exerted as she tried to control the shudder that ran through her. "He pulled the head off Molly McBright."

Hunter jumped to his feet and raced through the restaurant and out the door. If he could only catch this man, he'd have proof that someone was putting young children's lives in jeopardy by tampering with his dolls.

As he burst onto the sidewalk, he caught a glimpse of a black car streaking away. In the back seat window, Molly McBright's head looked at him. Then the car was gone.

"Damn." Hunter spun and looked in the other direction. The street was empty. "Double damn!" The man had evaded him. He returned to the restaurant and Sylvie, whose blue eyes lit up as she saw him approaching. Hunter swallowed. The woman had an effect on him—one he hadn't counted on. Just her look of relief at his return made him almost giddy. It was a foolish reaction, in light of the fact that he'd met her in a robbery attempt and knew nothing about her. Except that she believed in him, if only a tiny bit.

He shook his head. "He got away."

"At least he's gone." Sylvie rubbed her arms. "It's creepy. So what do they want?"

"I'm not sure," Hunter said. He wasn't positive, but he did have an idea. "About six months ago, when I registered the formula for the dolls for a patent, I had an offer to buy me out."

"Someone wanted the dolls?" Sylvie wasn't a businesswoman, but she saw potential here for a sabotage attempt. It was clear—another company wanted to put Hunter out of business.

"Not the dolls, they wanted the formula of the dolls."

"Which is what, exactly?" Sylvie asked. "I know from reading the box that they're soft and cuddly and filled with not only antibacterial substances but also vitamins and what amounts to a limited boost to certain vaccinations."

Hunter nodded. "I'm a doctor, not a chemist, but I was working with some herbs. Not a new concept," he said modestly. "But I found a combination of plants that actually work to build up the immune system in children who are malnourished. It isn't actually a vaccination, but it is highly effective in helping children fight off childhood diseases. My theory in creating the dolls was that if I could figure out a way to make them and distribute them to third-world countries, we could improve the overall health of children around the world."

What he expected to see on Sylvie's piquant face was skepticism. Instead, he saw a flash of pain so intense that he actually felt it himself. "What?"

Sylvie's face was white, but she didn't look away from him. "Two of my brothers died of whooping cough."

"There's a vaccina—" Hunter stopped. Sylvie knew that. He could see it in her face. She knew that her brothers had died because someone neglected to do the basics for them. "I'm sorry," he said.

"Those dolls will help third-world countries, but they'd also do a lot of good right here in New York City." She looked down at her hands. "I should have gotten their vaccinations. My mother was…ill a lot. I was supposed to make sure the babies got what they needed. And they got so sick."

Hunter saw her hands tremble, and he reached across the table and picked them up, folding them into his own. "They were your siblings, Sylvie. Not your children."

Her blue eyes were so clear and hot that Hunter felt blasted by her pain. "I was the only mother they had, and I let them down."

He held her hands tighter. "How old were you?"

She shook her head. "Age is irrelevant. I was in charge. I knew I could take them to the clinic. I just didn't do it. I was tired and trying to stay in school." She shrugged, forcing a smile. "One thing left undone. One task pushed back. The result is disaster. I think of all the things I did correctly, all of the cooking and laundry and making sure they made it to school safely. And the one thing I let slide was the most important thing of all."

Hunter understood the depth of Sylvie's pain, and

he knew that somehow she had to rise to the surface of it. He knew from personal experience. But how to help her was the question. He used his hands to hold her in the present, to keep her from spiraling back into the blackness of the past. "Sylvie, if you had taken them to the clinic, then that would have been the day that something else happened."

For an instant he saw the hope in her eyes—hope that she could forgive herself. He brought her hands up in his. He wanted to hold her. Not in a sexual way, though God knew he was attracted to her, but in solace and comfort.

"But I didn't take them," she whispered.

Hunter increased the pressure on her hands. "How old were you?" he asked again.

"Twelve."

He held her with his eyes. "You can't hold a twelve-year-old accountable. You wouldn't do it to a child of your own, and you can't do it to yourself."

He saw her lips tremble, and he thought for a moment she'd cry. But instead, the corners of her mouth turned up into a smile, and this time there was not even a trace of skepticism. He felt a strange pulling in his chest. Sylvie West, with her elfin features and tough exterior, was the most beautiful woman he'd ever seen.

Sylvie glanced up as the waiter brought their food. Hunter reluctantly released her hands as the dishes were placed on the table. He saw her composure regained, and he smiled encouragement at her.

While they ate, he kept the conversation light, and Familiar, under the table, added humor to the meal as they slipped portions of fish to him. When they were finished, Sylvie hid him inside her coat as they left.

Hunter hailed a cab, and they headed toward the toy store. In the back of the cab, he felt an irresistible urge to draw her closer to him, but he checked himself. He'd learned something valuable—her tough façade covered tremendous vulnerability. To tread on it could prove destructive to both of them.

"I can't thank you enough for what you're doing," he said.

"I don't expect thanks," she answered, but she took the sting out of her words with a smile. "I suspect you may be the second truly good person I've met in my entire life. Don't shatter my illusions, okay?"

He chuckled softly. "I'll do my best."

They got out of the cab at the back of the store, and Sylvie retrieved her keys. Once inside, she listened for a moment. "I'm not sure if they have a full-time security guard or not."

"We'll be very quiet and very quick," Hunter promised her.

She led him and the cat to the billing department. "I'm not much at computers," she admitted as she pointed to a bank of machinery.

Hunter scanned the room. He knew a bit about software, but he wasn't certain he could crack the billing codes. "Let's take a look."

He sat down at a computer and focused his attention on the job at hand. It took fifteen minutes to find the invoice code for the dolls, but once he did, it was only a matter of time until he found the sales records. He felt his stomach knot as he saw that one Buster and two Mollys had been sold. The Mollys were credit-card purchases, and he looked up the names easily. But the Buster had been a cash purchase. There was no record of the person who had bought the doll.

"What are you going to do?" Sylvie asked as she read over his shoulder.

"Get back the two I can find. They're both in the city, thank goodness. And with the Buster, I'll have to think of something."

He felt her hands on his shoulders, a light pressure of support. "I'm sorry," she said, whispering almost in his ear.

Hunter leaned back and found that his head rested against her breasts. When she didn't move away, he closed his eyes. "My intentions were so good. I only wanted to help."

He was surprised when he felt her lips brush over his forehead. He forced himself to hold steady, to allow her to continue whatever initiative she chose to take. He knew with certain knowledge that if he pressed, she would flee.

Her lips moved to the corner of his eye, a delicate kiss that was as tentative as a whisper. And then she shifted to his lips. Hunter could feel his heart pounding. Her lips were soft, and when she shifted around to his side, he couldn't help himself. His hands moved to her waist and lifted her onto his lap.

Sylvie gave no objection as he held her in his arms and slowly deepened the kiss.

SHE FELT AS IF a stranger had crawled inside her skin. The desire to kiss Hunter was overpowering— stronger even than her fear. She opened her mouth to him and slipped her arms around his neck to hold on tighter. She yielded completely to the passion his lips ignited and the thrill of his touch.

Long ago, she'd vowed never to lose herself in emotion. It was dangerous. But this time she couldn't stop herself. She didn't want to.

In Hunter's arms, she felt safe to allow herself the pleasures of his kiss. If she was wrong about him, the consequences would be painful—and possibly fatal. But she wasn't wrong. She recognized something in him that made her believe—in him, and in herself. And his kisses were like a drug. Sensation washed over her. She desired him, no doubt about it. But she also felt tenderness and a need to comfort him. All in all, it was remarkable. She felt as if the petals of her soul, long held tight, had slowly begun to open.

"Meow!" She felt sharp pricks in her shin. It was like coming out of a drug-induced stupor.

"Meow!" The pain increased until she broke the contact and caught her breath. Her eyes were still unfocused as she sat up slightly and looked down at the cat.

"Meow!" Familiar gave a big swat to her leg, claws extended. He meant to get her attention and fast.

"What?" Hunter asked in a voice that also sounded drugged.

"It's the cat," she said. "He wants something."

Hunter shifted, his gaze beginning to move around the room. Outside the door of the computer room he saw a dark shadow slide across the frosted glass.

"Someone's out there," he whispered, easing from the chair to the floor with Sylvie in his lap. "Be quiet," he urged.

Sylvie had no intention of making a sound as soon

as she saw the shadow on the glass. It eased past, then returned. Slowly, very slowly, the man's silhouette turned to face the computer room.

The breath hissed out of her as if she'd been punctured. They hadn't bothered to lock the door. No one was in the store. Or were they? It was Christmas—the busiest time of the year. Perhaps stock boys were at work. She'd never stayed after hours, so she couldn't be certain what occurred once the doors were locked.

"Security?" Hunter asked hopefully.

Sylvie bit her lip. "Maybe." Even as she said it, she knew it wasn't the truth. If the store had security men, they wouldn't skulk around the corridors. This was someone who didn't belong in the store. Someone looking for them.

She watched the silhouette turn toward the hallway and begin to move forward. It vanished from the glass. "Let's get out of here," she said.

She started forward, but Hunter's hand stopped her. "Wait," he said. "It could be a trap."

"What are we going to do?" Sylvie checked her watch. It was midnight. "We can't stay here. If he is hunting us, he'll come back."

Hunter shifted his gaze from her face down her body. "Is there a Santa tableau?"

She knew immediately what he was thinking. "No," she said emphatically. "No!"

"Sylvie, if we can make it into the store front, we'll be safer."

She had to agree with that statement. But she wasn't going to pretend to be a Santa's helper mannequin. She couldn't do it. And what about Hunter? He didn't have a costume.

Hunter seemed to take her silence for consent, because he stood up and pulled her to her feet. "What about the cat?" she asked.

"He'll be fine," Hunter said. "Now I have a plan."

She didn't like the sound of that. "Another kidnapping, perhaps?"

She knew she sounded sharp, but she couldn't help herself. They were in serious trouble, and she didn't have a lot of confidence in Hunter's plans, based on his blueprint for getting his toys back.

"You get set up, and then make a noise that draws the man in your direction. I'll ambush him. Maybe we can find out who he is and what he wants."

"Hunter, that's—"

"The only option we have," Hunter said. "I know it isn't a great plan. But if we get that information, maybe we can resolve this before any more children are injured."

She couldn't argue with that statement, though she didn't like his plan of action. If the man was armed, Hunter could be seriously injured. Even killed. Ambushing was something best left to trained professionals. Hunter was anything but a martial arts expert.

"Couldn't we just try to sneak out of here and come up with a safer plan?" she asked.

Hunter shook his head. "We have today and tomorrow left to find those toys. Sunday morning some child is going to open their presents from Santa and possibly get very, very sick. I'd risk a lot to prevent that from happening."

As much as she didn't want to agree, she knew Hunter was right. There wasn't time to plan and hope that another opportunity would appear. It was now or never.

"Okay," she agreed. "I'll go to the second-floor display of giant blocks. It's like a child's castle. We had a Santa sitting in it yesterday, so it's arranged for a person. I'll topple a few blocks and see if I can get the guy's attention. You can get on the escalator. It isn't turned on, so you can wait at the top, and when he comes over, you can jump him." It was the best place in the entire store.

Hunter nodded. "Just be careful. Once you hear him coming, strike a pose and freeze."

"I know how to be a mannequin," she said wearily. "I just never realized I could be talked into being a dummy. This is nuts."

"Meow," Familiar agreed, but he stepped in front of them and led the way to the second-floor display.

Sylvie climbed among the brightly colored blocks, feeling Hunter's eyes on her the entire time. When she finally settled into a thronelike chair, she looked up to find him smiling at her. He didn't say anything. He didn't have to. He wore his feelings on his face, and she saw that he was proud of her. It was such a strange reaction that Sylvie felt herself blush. Before she could try to signal him, she heard something on the far side of the room. Hunter heard it, too, and ducked up the unmoving escalator. She glanced around, but the cat was nowhere in sight.

Sylvie listened carefully, but now the store was silent. Whoever it was had either stopped or grown more cautious. He wasn't making any noise at all. The full impact of what she and Hunter were doing struck her—and she didn't have to pretend to be frozen. She felt as if her heart had stopped. She was paralyzed by fear. Her hands gripped the arms of her chair and she held on to keep from fainting. Now wasn't the time for weakness, she scolded herself.

When the first wave of terror passed, she was able to once again concentrate on the noises in the store. She'd never been so aware of toys that ticked and tocked or the vague computer sounds of some of the games that continued to run even when the store was closed.

She had a wild moment remembering in ''The Nutcracker'' when all of the toys came to life. She let her eyes move from side to side and was glad that she and Hunter had selected the area for toddlers. A living, breathing Barney wouldn't be nearly as scary as the Jurassic Park display for older children. Or God forbid, a roomful of perfect-figure Barbies.

It was finally her sense of humor that gave her back her courage. When she heard three distinct footsteps on the other side of the room, she tipped over a block and let it fall, just as Hunter had instructed. She was, after all, the bait.

She saw the man coming long before he even looked her way. She was shocked to see that, because she was sitting in the midst of a toy display, he perceived her as a toy. He walked right by her and never gave a second glance. And he was headed straight toward the escalator and Hunter.

Hunter's plan hadn't been brilliant, but it looked as if it might actually work. To keep the man distracted, she nudged another block. It made a soft sound as it rolled on its side.

The man whirled, and Sylvie had a hard time controlling the scream that threatened to rise in her throat. He was holding a gun, and he swung the barrel back and forth as if he would shoot anything that dared to move.

She froze her features and stared unseeingly in front of her. She couldn't watch as the gun barrel found her as the target, then gradually moved on. She couldn't even breathe. She could only pray that she looked like a fake elf in toyland.

She could sense the man studying her. She'd over-played her hand and drawn his attention too closely. She should have been content to leave well enough alone. But she'd had to push the second block.

He took a step toward her, and out of the corner of her eye she could see his puzzled expression. He looked as if he saw something that he didn't quite believe. Something that he didn't trust his vision on. And he kept walking toward her. Sylvie knew then that the setup was over. Hunter would have to make a leap of at least six feet—and he'd better jump soon. The barrel of the man's gun was coming up and lev-eling off right at her heart.

A noise on the escalator made her look up. She was just in time to see Hunter's body toppling back-ward down the steel stairs.

''So, Dr. Semmes,'' a tall thin man said as he came down the escalator. ''It would seem that you aren't in a very good position to negotiate.''

Chapter Six

Hunter was unprepared for the blow to his head. He'd been watching the man in the overcoat approach Sylvie, and he'd never thought that there might be two of them in the store.

When the first blow fell across the back of his skull, he realized that he'd miscalculated terribly. The momentum of the blow threw him forward, and his precarious balance on the escalator was destroyed. Pitching head over heels down the steep decline, he grunted with the impact each time he landed, but his bruises weren't his primary concern. He'd left Sylvie defenseless in a store with two men he believed to be brutal. He'd let her down.

At the bottom of the escalator he shook his head in an effort to clear his senses. He was slightly stunned, and his body felt nothing—yet. He turned to look for Sylvie and was just in time to see the overcoat man grasping her arm and pulling her out of the toy blocks. Red, yellow and blue blocks scattered as Sylvie put up a fight.

"Take your hands off me, you creep," she said, kicking him in the shins with her elf boots.

"Settle down or I'll make it a point to teach you a lesson you won't forget."

Hunter struggled to his hands and knees and fought a wave of dizziness. He launched himself forward but something snared his leg and pulled him so that he landed flat on his stomach.

"Grab her," the thin man ordered as he stepped over Hunter's prone body.

"I'm not going anywhere." Sylvie followed her statement with a well-connected jab to her assailant's throat. The overcoat man reeled backward, choking.

Hunter was close enough to grab his leg. With grim determination he drew himself forward until he could bite down on the man's calf.

Overcoat shrieked and began dancing, and Hunter let loose and rolled before the man toppled to the floor. When overcoat hit, he lost his breath, and Hunter picked up a toy truck and brought it down with force on the man's skull. He jerked once and lay still.

The thin man stepped forward, and when Hunter saw the gun, he dropped the truck.

"You're not easily convinced to cooperate," the thin man said as he motioned for Sylvie to join him.

"Leave her alone," Hunter said. His body had recovered sensation and he suspected every bone might be broken, but he forced himself into a sitting position. He glanced at her and saw how she fought against showing her fear. He suddenly understood that she'd had a lot of practice at not showing fear. And yet she'd agreed to help him—knowing it might be dangerous. "Sylvie—"

"I'm okay," she said, and Hunter thought he

would trade anything in his life never to have involved her in his problems.

"She's okay for now," the thin man said as he nudged his companion with the toe of his polished shoe and got no response. "But she won't be for long unless you listen to me."

"What do you want?" Hunter grabbed the escalator rail and pulled himself to his feet. He was battered but nothing was broken.

"I think you know the answer to that," the man said, and there was a trace of an accent in his tone. "I want the formula for the dolls."

"It isn't worth a penny," Hunter said. "The dolls are making children sick."

"Of course they are," the man said. "There's nothing wrong with the product though, it's simply the wrong company producing it."

Hunter clenched his hands in anger. "You're admitting that you tampered with the formula. That you deliberately did something that caused serious illness in those children."

"All's fair in love and war," the man said in a mocking tone. "And when there's this much money involved, this is definitely war."

"Who are you?" Hunter asked.

"I'm nobody. But I represent an interested party. And let me put this as clearly as I can. My client is going to have your formula, no matter the cost. There seems to be a market for your…endeavors." The man laughed as if he'd made a joke.

"These dolls aren't intended to make money—" Hunter said.

"You're an idiot," the thin man said coolly. "I

was warned that you think you're some noble, heroic figure. I didn't believe anyone could be so naive.''

The contempt was so clear in the man's voice that Hunter felt as if he'd been struck. Before he could answer, Sylvie spoke up.

''You're like every piece of scum I grew up with,'' she said, eyes so crystal-blue they looked as if they would shatter. ''Every hell pit in the world is controlled by someone like you. I spit on you.''

The man laughed openly. ''My, my, you are a feisty little thing, aren't you? And so cute in that costume. The doctor certainly has an eye for comely assistants.''

Hunter started forward, but the thin man grasped Sylvie's arm and twisted it hard. ''Stay back or I'll be forced to hurt her,'' he said. ''Make sure you haven't seriously damaged my friend there,'' he said, indicating the overcoat man.

Hunter bent to check the man he'd bashed on the head. ''He's unconscious. I'd check for a concussion,'' he said, unable to withhold his best medical advice, even for a criminal.

''Wake him,'' the thin man ordered.

Hunter hesitated. As it was, he had a chance against one man. He knelt beside the prone man and pretended to try and wake him. ''I'd call an ambulance,'' he said at last. ''If it is a concussion, then he needs to be stabilized.''

''I'm afraid I'll have to leave him to your tender mercies,'' the thin man said. ''Miss West and I have an appointment. And I'm sure as long as I'm entertaining your little friend, you won't do anything stupid like call the cops.''

Hunter rose swiftly, but the gun pointed at Sylvie's ribs stopped him.

"Don't do anything heroic," the thin man said. "She's going with me. I don't intend to harm her, unless you make me. Do you understand?"

Hunter understood perfectly. Sylvie was a hostage. All because she'd tried to help him. He nodded.

"Now let me give you a brief glimpse of the future," the thin man said. "Miss West and I will leave. In two hours, you'll go to the phone booth at the corner of Third and Thirty-fourth street. The phone will ring and then you'll be told where to leave the formula for the dolls."

"But I—"

The thin man shook his head as he raised the gun barrel to Sylvie's temple. "No arguing, Dr. Semmes. Do as you're told, and this young woman won't be injured. Disobey, and she will suffer. And I'm sure you've learned tonight about three recent purchases—including one doll that was bought with cash. Remember that particular doll?" His smile was wolfish. "The other dolls contain something that produces illness. That doll is different. Shall we say, more *potent*."

Hunter felt his stomach knot, and he saw the look of worry that flashed across Sylvie's face before she controlled it. She was tough. When she turned to the thin man, her voice was filled with disgust. "If you want to make money from the formula, don't you think it would be stupid to let a kid die?"

Hunter could have kissed her. The thin man lifted his shoulders. "I don't make the plans, my dear, I merely carry them out. I'm sure my boss has covered all contingencies. Besides, it isn't something you should worry your pretty little head about.'' His voice deepened. ''You have plenty of real worries of your own.'' He shot Hunter a meaningful look. ''I'll hurt her if I have to,'' he said.

Hunter believed him. ''I promise you, if you do, I'll find you wherever you go. And no matter what my personal beliefs are against harming another person, I will kill you.'' He had stepped beyond a boundary in his life, one he'd never thought to cross.

The thin man narrowed his gaze on Hunter for a split second before he spoke. ''Well, I must bid you adieu. Because you are such a good soul, I'm sure that you'll see that Alto gets medical care. Don't call an ambulance or the cops. We wouldn't want this little incident brought to the attention of the authorities.''

Hunter swallowed. ''Take me instead of Sylvie. I'll take you to the formula.''

''No, that isn't going to work. We feel you'll be more willing to cooperate to save her than yourself,'' the thin man said.

He grasped Sylvie's elbow and pushed her in front of him toward the back exit. When she didn't move fast enough, he pushed again. ''Don't try to drag your feet,'' he said roughly as he put his hand in her back and shoved.

Hunter started forward, then stopped himself. He couldn't risk Sylvie getting hurt. And he believed the thin man would shoot her.

''The formula is no good if people perceive the dolls to be dangerous,'' he said.

''That isn't your worry any longer, Dr. Semmes,'' the man said, pushing Sylvie again. ''Just do what you're told.''

Hunter waited until they were out of sight before he started after them. He tried to remember someplace in the store where he could stage an ambush. But he could hardly remember his way around. They had to go through the *Star Trek* display to get to the stairwell, he remembered that. After the *Wizard of Oz* set! There was one place where he might be able to use the element of surprise to his benefit. He cut through toy displays and headed for the yellow brick road.

Hunter had just positioned himself when he saw Sylvie step around a display of radios. The thin man was smiling cruelly, and he said something that made Sylvie twist around to confront him.

"I'm only surprised that something as slimy as you evolved to have legs," Sylvie said.

"You talk big now," the man said with some temper. "You'd better watch yourself or you'll give away your guttersnipe background. Does the good doctor know the type of person he's taken up with?" The man's slight accent was completely gone—his dialect now distinctly that of one of the New York boroughs. And the man spoke to Sylvie with a degree of familiarity that made Hunter frown.

He listened closely, thinking maybe he'd misunderstood. Was it possible that the thin man knew Sylvie?

"He doesn't care about my background," Sylvie said hotly. "It isn't an issue."

"It would be if he knew."

They were drawing closer, and Hunter crouched low. He would have to count on the momentum of his body to knock the other man completely down. The good thing was that Sylvie's attitude had made the man careless with the gun. He was no longer pointing it at her.

Hunter knew if he acted quickly and with full force, he'd be able to hold the thin man down while Sylvie made a getaway.

"You'd better pray none of those children die," Sylvie said as they drew ever closer.

"It isn't my worry—I'm not the medical man in all of this. Besides, Dr. Semmes will bear the brunt of any deaths. He's the inventor." The man laughed out loud.

Hunter saw his moment, but before he could move, a flash of black arced through the air and landed directly on top of the thin man's head.

"Familiar!" he whispered.

The black cat hung on tight with all four claws, sending the thin man into a wild and thrashing dance.

Sylvie drew back her foot and delivered a series of well-placed kicks. "You creep!" she said as she brought her heel down sharply on his right arch.

The man hopped one-legged closer and closer to Hunter as he tried to pull the cat off him. But Familiar was hooked in tight. Hunter grabbed the man's hand and took the gun.

"Meow!" Familiar cried.

"Let's get out of here," Sylvie said, grasping Hunter's hand. "We can pull the fire alarm on the way out and hope the cops get here before they make an escape."

"We need to find out who they work for," Hunter said, hesitating.

"He's not going to tell you beans," Sylvie assured him. "And we don't have time to waste. We have to get out of here before we're caught. The cops will take all of us to jail and worry about sorting it out later.''

Hunter listened to her and knew she was right, but he was afraid if he let the men get away, he'd never find out who was behind the plot to ruin him—or how to find the doll.

"We can hide outside and follow them!" Sylvie said, pushing at Hunter to get him moving. "Come on. The cat's going to get tired of whirling around in a circle and have to let go."

"We can't leave Familiar—"

"Trust me, that cat will be right on our heels as soon as we hit the door," Sylvie said.

Hunter hesitated for another second, then grabbed Sylvie's hand, and together they ran for the back exit. At the rear door Sylvie smashed the glass on the fire alarm with her elf boot and pulled the handle. "I hope they put them in jail," she said as she flew out into the alley with Hunter at her side. Before the door could close, a black shadow shot through and Familiar leaped into Hunter's arms.

"Thanks, cat," he said.

"I'll say," Sylvie said, scratching the cat's head before she ran to the corner and hailed a cab.

"Take us to—" She looked at Hunter.

"Just ease up the corner," Hunter directed. "We're waiting for someone."

The cabby shrugged a shoulder. "The meter's running."

They sat parked for ten minutes before they heard the sound of a fire truck screaming toward them.

Hunter felt Sylvie's gaze on him as she snuggled the cat inside her coat. No one had come out of the building. Or at least not out the door they'd used for an exit.

"What should we do?" Sylvie asked softly. The fire truck pulled into the ally they'd just left and firemen swarmed out. "If they're still in there, they'll be arrested," Hunter said with an edge of satisfaction.

"We can check at the police station later tonight," Sylvie said.

Hunter looked at her. "How?"

"Check the docket." Sylvie gave a rueful smile. "The neighborhood I grew up in, I had a lot of practice learning about how the police system works."

"I don't suppose there's any reason to hang around here." Hunter saw a fireman staring at the idling cab. "We should go." He tapped the glass partition. "Thirty-fourth Street," he said.

The cab pulled away with a screech of tires and Hunter caught Sylvie as she was thrown against him. The feel of her was like a match to kindling, and he had to restrain himself from kissing her. He felt her straighten and said nothing. There was so much at stake—and now he had the terrible feeling that his heart was also at risk.

SYLVIE WANDERED AROUND the toy counter, picking up wooden wagons or spool toys, all carefully carved and brightly painted.

"Did you always want to be a doctor?" she asked. She was worried about him. He'd taken the two addresses they'd obtained for the families who had purchased the dolls and he was mapping out the locations. He'd been extremely quiet ever since they'd left the toy store.

She paced along the counter, wondering if he regretted the kisses they'd shared. Or did he even remember?

"I always wanted to be able to fix things," he said. He started to add something but stopped.

"What?" she asked, moving closer to him. She felt as if a wall had been erected between them and for just a second she'd felt it begin to crumble.

"My mother wasn't well. She was sick a lot when I was growing up, and no one could help her." He smoothed the map with strong, sure hands. "Then when Brad got sick, it was like the same nightmare again."

Sylvie wanted to go to him, to put her arms around him and offer what small comfort she could. But she was afraid to do it. He'd been so distant. She knew what it was like not to want others to intrude on private pain.

Her hesitation cost her the moment. Hunter straightened up and began to pace. "We have to get those dolls back."

Sylvie did have something she could offer for comfort in that area. "That won't be hard," she said, grinning.

"I don't relish the idea of breaking into two different apartments, one in a very secure building, I might add."

Sylvie's grin widened. "We don't have to break in."

"How are we going to get the dolls?"

Hunter's eyes held hope and doubt. And she couldn't help but smile even wider. "We call them up and say there's a problem with the dolls. We offer them double money back or any substitute they want from your shop.''

Hunter looked up at the ceiling. ''You are a genius!'' He went to her and put his hands on her shoulders. ''You have more sense than most people I know all rolled together.''

Sylvie felt the blush start at her neck and rise swiftly to her face. She wasn't used to such unqualified praise, especially not about her brain power. ''Thanks, but it was just common sense.''

He smiled down at her. ''It was a lot more than common sense. You and that cat...'' He looked over at the sleeping Familiar, who'd curled up with a large, stuffed calico cat.

''Now, the cat is truly amazing,'' Sylvie agreed.

''And you are, too.''

This time when she looked into Hunter's eyes, she saw the flicker of passion that she thought had disappeared. ''We can call them first thing in the morning. In fact, I'll call as the secretary of your company. I'll say that the doll's hair might come loose and you're recalling the product until you make certain it's safe.''

She saw that he heard what she said, but she also saw that his response to her was on another level. She swallowed. She was playing with fire with Hunter Semmes. He wasn't like any other man she'd ever known. He genuinely cared about others. And maybe he did want to be Batman or Superman or some heroic figure. Was there anything wrong with that? Lots of the boys and men she'd grown up with were so busy trying to survive, they never had time to dream.

''You're remarkable,'' Hunter said.

The air between them seemed superheated. Sylvie felt it warm her entire body as she took a ragged breath. Her response to Hunter frightened her. Just looking into his eyes made her want him. And she'd known him for less than a day. It didn't make sense. It went against all of the cautious rules she'd made up to protect herself from the harsh realities of life.

She found she had nothing to say to him, yet she couldn't look away. She lifted her face and waited for his kiss.

He bent toward her, and she put her arms around his neck. When their lips connected, she knew there was no middle ground here, no weighing of odds. Once they began to kiss, she knew that whatever the risk, she'd take it.

Hunter must have read her acquiescence in her body. He broke the kiss and put his hands on her face. "Are you certain?" he asked.

She nodded, her heart pounding so hard she didn't think she could talk.

He took her hand and led her to the elevator. Once inside he pushed the button the to third floor. "As I told you before, it isn't a penthouse," he said with a slight smile. "But I have a funny feeling that it won't matter where we are."

As the elevator started up, he pulled her into his arms and began to kiss her again.

Chapter Seven

Sylvie was not aware of the room Hunter led her to. There was only Hunter, his kisses, his hands moving over her, stoking the fire in her blood. The bed was large and soft, and she sank into it with him.

He undressed her slowly, taking his time as he revealed her body to the dim light that filtered through large windows.

She watched his face, wanting to remember every detail. She felt as if she'd stepped into a world that she'd never believed existed. A fairy tale. A place of magic and wonder. These were the scenes she'd watched in movies and scoffed at. But it was happening, and her feelings for Hunter were so strong that she never doubted the rightness of being with him.

"You're beautiful," he said as he ran his hand over her breasts and down her stomach.

She reached up and unbuttoned his shirt, pushing it off his shoulders. She was eager for the feel of his skin against her yet she also wanted to linger. She had learned the valuable lesson long ago of making the good things last. To savor the rare moment of pure pleasure.

Hunter's hands moved over her, his lips following, and Sylvie knew that she couldn't wait much longer. She captured his face and drew him down to her and gave herself to the pleasure of making love with him.

SO THE DOC AND THE SPRITE have gone upstairs on a cold December night. I can't think of a better thing for either of them. It's amazing in this city of twelve million that there are so many lonely folks. But as the old television show used to say, "There are a million stories in the naked city." I always loved that tagline.

I'm delighted Sylvie and Hunter have found each other, but I don't think I've ever met two people more fragile when it comes to the romantic tango. I hope they don't overextend. Love is an addictive emotion—all that flushing and rushing of hot feeling. Then fear sets in, and I can see where both of these humanoids are loaded to the gills with insecurities and doubts. It could get pretty rocky as one or the other scrambles for safety.

But only time will tell. Familiar, the master of matchmaking, is on the scene. I'll do my best to help them steer a straight course through the rocky shoals of love.

Yikes, I'm beginning to sound like a really bad television show. I'd better turn my attention to the more critical problem at hand. How to find the one doll. That's assuming that the deadly duo we left behind in the store weren't lying. But they knew exactly how many dolls had been purchased and that two were paid for with credit cards.

Which brings me to several important points. Is

there someone in the store working with the criminals? Or were all the purchases setups?

The problem is, thin man implied that one doll was laced with something more deadly than the others. Now, whether he was bluffing or not, I can't say. Humans are capable of almost anything. When I take my strolls in the capital, I pass houses where families are gathered around the television oohing and aahing as they watch a nature show about tigers or wolves. They are amazed at the skill these creatures have to hunt and survive. They find the hunters of the natural world to be cruel and brutal.

Then I pop into a movie and in the first ten minutes, I see people shot, stabbed, run over, blown up, drowned, poisoned, bludgeoned, tortured, burned and stomped. Now tell me which species has got the market cornered on violence.

Enough deep thinking—time to turn to the problem at hand. I have only two clues to work with. The thin man spoke with a foreign accent, slight but distinct. And then when he thought he was alone with Sylvie, that accent disappeared and he sounded like a native New Yorker.

He also made it clear he was working for someone else. Someone who knew a lot about Hunter's business—and something about Sylvie's background. Someone already in the toy business, perhaps. While the lovebirds are busy, I'll flip through the yellow pages and see what I can find in the way of toy manufacturers in this area. It's a long shot but since I'm a nocturnal creature, I might as well put my time to good use.

THE FIRST LIGHT OF DAWN filtered in through the big window, and Sylvie woke up with the strangest sense of safety. One of Hunter's arms was her pillow and the other was thrown across her shoulders, pulling her into his body.

She was facing the large arched window that spilled the pinkish light of dawn across the bed. Outside the window she could see the light changing the colors on the old brick buildings that made up Hunter's neighborhood.

She felt his light breathing on the top of her head, and closed her eyes. It had been a long time since she'd let anyone get this close to her. In fact, she'd decided never to put herself in a position to trust another human being again. And yet Hunter had broken down those barriers without even knowing he'd assaulted them. He was so willing to trust her. And he'd suffered a few body slams himself.

She shifted in his arms so she could study his face. He was heartbreakingly handsome, though he didn't seem to know it. His jaw was strong, his face lean and sculpted. But it was his eyes and lips that fascinated her. Dark lashes were closed over his brown eyes, but she had already memorized the color and intensity. His eyes showed his feelings, and what she'd seen of them made her believe that he was a man capable of deep commitment.

She saw his eyelashes flutter and open. His first reaction was a slow smile. "I was afraid I'd dreamed last night," he said, gently brushing her black hair away from her pale cheek.

"I think it really happened," she said, smiling back. He made her feel as if she was brand-new, something shiny and wonderful. It struck her suddenly that he made her feel like the best present he'd ever received.

"I wish I knew the formula to be able to hold on to last night and make it last forever." He kissed her forehead. "On the other hand, it would certainly ruin my work ethic."

Sylvie laughed. She hadn't given a thought to going to work. Since she'd met Hunter, she felt as if she'd been yanked up and plopped down on another planet.

"You don't have to punch a time clock, but I do. I have to be at work by nine." She opened her eyes wider. "And I have a date for lunch."

Even though she said it lightly, she saw Hunter's eyebrows draw together. The idea that he was jealous over her sent another rush of pleasure through her. "It's with that elderly gentleman who rescued me yesterday. Mr. Fenton. He's playing Santa at St. Mary's Orphanage and I'm going to help him out as an elf."

Hunter's face relaxed. "That's a wonderful thing to do."

"He seems like a terrific old man." She brushed her fingers across Hunter's cheek and felt the beginning of his beard. "But it isn't even seven yet." Her voice dropped slightly and she saw that he immediately caught her meaning.

"Let's see, I can get up and make us some breakfast," he said with a hint of teasing in his voice.

"I was never a breakfast eater," she answered.

"As a doctor, I have to tell you that breakfast is the most important meal." He nibbled at her ear.

"Let's do toast in an hour," she answered, sliding a hand down his ribs.

"I see your point," he whispered as he began to kiss her.

HUNTER WATCHED as Sylvie dressed in the morning light. The elf costume was all she had, and he laughed at her face as she slipped it over her head.

"I'll drive you to your place so you can change," he offered.

"I can take a cab. It'll be quicker." She checked her watch. "And I'd better be quick."

Hunter rose. "I'm sorry, I didn't—"

"I'm not sorry about a darn thing," Sylvie added, reaching over to put her fingers on his lips. "Nothing except that I have to go."

"I'd ask you to lunch, but I know you have other plans."

"And you need to contact those families with the dolls and retrieve them."

Hunter let his fingers glide through her silky hair. "I'm worried that something will happen to you at work." He had the strongest urge not to let her out of his sight.

"I'll be fine," she reassured him. "I know what to watch out for now. Trust me, I won't be caught by surprise twice."

Hunter wanted to hold her, but he stepped back. "Sylvie, when the tall, thin man was taking you out of the building, he said something as if he knew you. Did you know him?"

He saw something glint in her eyes, then disappear.

"I know his type. I grew up with muscle for hire." She shrugged and bent to retrieve her boots. "I have to go now.'' She slipped her feet in the boots and started toward the door.

Hunter felt a pang of concern. ''Did I upset you?''

She halted, then slowly turned to face him. ''My past is my business,'' she said slowly. ''If it matters to you that I grew up poor and in rough company, you'd better decide now.''

Her attitude was a shock to Hunter. ''Hey,'' he said, starting forward, ''I didn't mean—''

''We come from two different worlds. I knew that, even if you didn't. This,'' she swept her hand around, ''this is a way of life I knew existed, but it isn't how I grew up.''

''Sylvie, this doesn't matter. What matters is who you are inside.''

For the first time in hours, he saw the bitterness back in her face. ''You're not foolish enough to believe that. Money matters. Background matters. What we both have to decide is how much it matters.'' She shook her head. ''I'm sorry, I have to go now.''

He started to stop her, but thought better of it. His question had triggered an emotional reaction. It would be better to let her work through it and talk it out later. And she did have to go to work. As sensitive as she was, he didn't want to do anything that might imply to her that he didn't respect her job.

He went to the window and watched as she hailed a cab and jumped into it. He felt as if something very important had just exited his life.

He showered and dressed and went downstairs. Within the hour he'd spoken with both doll owners and had worked out a trade. All he had to do was drive across town and make the exchange.

The third doll was still out there, though. Even as

he got his keys and held the door of his car for the cat, he gnawed at the problem of the missing doll.

He opted to drive his old Volvo, fearing that police would still be on the lookout for his van. And the Volvo bore the license plates that showed him to be a doctor—a possible edge when convincing parents of his sincerity.

The cat jumped into the front passenger seat, paws on the dash if he were standing lookout on a ship. "Maybe we'll stop by St. Mary's," Hunter said more to himself than the cat.

"Meow," Familiar agreed.

"It's a date then. Let's get these dolls back and run some tests." He felt a bit of hope as he headed into the dense Christmas traffic.

SYLVIE BAGGED THE TOYS for the Christmas shopper and offered a smile.

"Merry Christmas," the woman said.

"The same to you," Sylvie answered.

She looked up to see Alice staring at her. "What?" she asked.

"That actually sounded as if you meant it. I thought you hated Christmas."

Sylvie lifted a shoulder. They'd been so busy she hadn't had a chance to think about anything. "Maybe it isn't as bad as I thought."

"My, my, my," Alice said, eyebrows arching. "You get abducted at gunpoint yesterday, you come back all doctored up and deny the whole incident—which, by the way, I saw with my own two eyes—and now you're actually smiling and giving out Christmas greetings to the public. Something is happening here. Something big. If I had to guess I'd say you'd met a member of the opposite sex.''

Sylvie laughed, though she had to force it. ''You say that about everything, Alice. If I order dessert you think I'm dating someone. If I order a salad, you think I'm loosing weight to impress someone.''

Alice waved a hand in the air, dismissing all of Sylvie's statements. ''This is different. *You're* different. You are…glowing.''

''Pregnant women glow,'' Sylvie said, then instantly regretted her choice of words.

''They glow because they've been doing what's required to get pregnant,'' Alice said with a laugh. ''You act as though it's a crime to meet someone you like. I'm happy for you. And it couldn't happen at a better time of year than Christmas.''

For some reason Sylvie felt compelled to deny that anything had happened, but she clamped her mouth shut. Protesting too much would only make Alice worse. And she had enough worries. At the top of the list was her reaction to Hunter's simple question.

He hadn't implied that she knew the thin man—not personally. What troubled Sylvie was that she *had* known him, or rather plenty just like him. And he'd recognized that in her, even if Hunter had not. Hunter Semmes was a man who lived in a world of ideals. He was a good man because he believed in goodness. But she'd never had the luxury of goodness.

''World to Sylvie, world to Sylvie,'' Alice said, jostling her elbow.

Sylvie looked up to find a mother, her arms loaded with presents and her child hanging on her skirt. ''Could I get these gift wrapped?'' the woman asked.

"Certainly," Sylvie said, glad for once that the Christmas rush would keep her too busy to worry much more.

She finished the gift wrapping, and out of the corner of her eye she saw the police officers headed her way. "Oh, no," she said softly. "Here comes trouble."

Alice nodded. "Don't worry."

The two policemen nodded at Alice but zeroed in on Sylvie. "We've been looking for you," one officer said. "You were abducted yesterday at gunpoint, weren't you?" His eyes narrowed as he scrutinized her. "Do you know anything about the break-in last night?"

"Yes. No. Uh—I was abducted. I didn't know the store was broken into." Sylvie stumbled over the words.

"Where were you last night?" the second policeman asked. "We had someone watching your apartment and you never went home."

Sylvie felt as if a large hand clutched her neck, pressing hard. She suddenly felt trapped.

"Sylvie was with me," Alice said, pushing herself between Sylvie and the officers. "She was abducted yesterday by a man she'd never seen before and doesn't know. He released her and she got medical attention. After the horror of that event, she went to my place, and last night I took care of her. Right now you're not doing anything to make it easier for her, so if you don't have a warrant for her arrest, I suggest you back off and look for criminals, not harass innocent citizens."

The two officers didn't step back, but their aggressive attitudes changed. "You were with her all night?" they asked Alice.

"All night. I want to point out to you that she's a victim here, not a criminal. If this is your idea of protecting—"

"Sorry, ma'am," they said. The first one turned back to Sylvie. "If you think of anything that might help us identify the man who abducted you, we'd appreciate the help. The store has hired some additional security guards for the safety of the employees and customers. We'll be working with them."

"Certainly," Sylvie managed to say.

She watched in amazement as they walked away. Her experience with authority figures had never been so smooth.

"Thanks," she whispered to Alice.

"Don't mention it."

Several customers appeared at the counter, and there was no time to talk. When they'd checked out three other customers, Alice looked at her watch. "What's on your agenda for lunch?" she asked.

Sylvie realized it was eleven-thirty. The morning was gone. "I have to do something," she said mysteriously, and at the expectancy in Alice's face, she had a sudden inspiration. Alice was nearing retirement, a woman who'd worked hard and with good spirit all of her life. "Why don't you join me for lunch?" Sylvie asked.

"In the café?"

"Nope," Sylvie said, unable to suppress her grin. "At St. Mary's Orphanage. I'm helping Santa Claus today."

"I don't believe it. The Grinch is volunteering to

distribute Christmas spirit. Whoever this guy is you've met, I want to meet him.''

"His name is Chester Fenton," Sylvie said, certain that she was on to a good idea. "You're going to love him."

"Let me grab my coat," she said, eyeing Sylvie's costume. "How many of those did they give you?"

"Give me? Get a grip. They made me buy one for every workday."

"I'm ready whenever you are," Alice said.

Together they clocked out and headed into the street. Neither of them saw the man in the brown overcoat, hat pulled low, grab the cab behind them and follow.

HUNTER PARKED IN THE LOT of the orphanage. He grabbed a box of presents from the trunk, but he knew that the black cat would be a bigger hit for the boys and girls than any of the toys he'd brought along. And that was fine by him.

He'd retrieved the two dolls without difficulty, and he'd checked again at the precinct jail, just as Sylvie had told him. No one had been arrested in the false fire alarm at the toy store. He'd checked the morning paper and found a small article about the false alarm and minor damage in the store. Police were investigating.

Familiar walked at his side as they went up the steps and into the back offices of the old and respected orphanage. This was his fifth year of bringing gifts. He always left them for the staff to hand out. Today he was eager to see the Santa—and more especially, the elf.

He left the presents and followed one of the staffers down the corridor to the central meeting room where a big tree had been decorated and the children eagerly waited. He watched the faces of the children, seeing hope and sadness and excitement. He knew in his heart that there should be at least one day in each year when a child's wishes came true. He only wished he had the power to make it so.

He took a seat among a group of children and listened to them talk about past Christmases. He caught the infectious excitement as they waited for Santa. His gaze fell on a young girl who looked no more than six. She sat alone and quietly brushed tears from her eyes.

Hunter didn't hesitate. He went to her and knelt beside her. "Are you okay?"

She nodded, wiping away another tear. "I want my mama."

There was no answer to that request. Hunter picked her up and held her in his arms. "I think Santa is about to arrive," he said, hoping to distract her. "What's your name?"

"Melanie," she said softly. "Melanie Mull. My mama got sick and died. I had to come here, but I want to go home."

"What about your father?" Hunter asked, feeling helpless to do anything for the child.

"He went away. It was a long time ago." The child put her hand in Hunter's hair. "I don't miss him. But I miss Mama."

"I had a little boy, but he died. I miss him a lot, too."

The child turned big, sad eyes up at him. "I'm sorry."

He forced a smile. "Me, too."

"Maybe Santa will have a present for you," she said.

"I think my present is getting to meet you, Miss Melanie Mull."

Her tiny face seemed to glow with her smile. "I think you're a nice man." Suddenly she saw the black cat. "Is he yours? Can I pet him?"

Hunter didn't have to answer. Familiar hopped into the little girl's arms. The door opened and the best Santa Hunter had ever seen came through. Right on his heels was Sylvie, smiling like he'd never seen her smile before. And following them was one of the women he remembered from the toy store.

Hunter put Melanie on her feet so she could join the other children as they rushed to climb on Santa's lap. He drew back into a corner of the room and watched as one by one, Santa lifted the children and listened to their whispers of Christmas wishes.

As Santa heard the wishes, he called out to Sylvie to add them to her list.

Hunter was charmed by the scene, and as the Santa listened to the last child, he stepped forward. He caught Sylvie's eye and saw a flush climb up her cheeks.

The older woman at her elbow laughed out loud as she gave Hunter the eye. "So this is the man who's put the mistletoe back in Christmas for you. I must say, I heartily approve of your taste, Sylvie West."

Chapter Eight

Sylvie was shocked to see Hunter, but that reaction swiftly gave way to pleasure. And she could tell that Alice strongly approved. Who wouldn't? Hunter was a handsome man.

She watched as her co-worker shook Hunter's hand. Alice was the grandmotherly type, but she was nobody's fool. It would be good to get her assessment of the man who had turned her life upside down.

Chester Fenton was also showing more than a little interest in Hunter. "So you're the inventor?" he said, taking Hunter's hand.

Sylvie did a double take. She'd never mentioned anything about Hunter to the older man.

"I read about you in a magazine," Chester said, beaming at Hunter, then glancing at Sylvie before he turned back to Hunter. "This doll of yours is a remarkable idea. How are sales going?"

Hunter maintained a cool composure. "The doll has drawn some unusual interest," he said. "I'm hoping to learn more anyday."

"Excellent," Chester said as he ushered them out of the room with the children and down a long cor-

ridor. "It's a tradition here that after the Santa visit,
I stop down the hall for a moment with some of the
children who were too sick to attend. You don't
mind, do you?" He looked at Alice and Hunter, waiting for their approval. He already knew Sylvie's answer.

"Miss West and I will return in ten minutes,"
Chester said. "I know the two of you have to get
back to work," he said, directing the last comment
to Alice.

When Chester opened the door, Sylvie entered the
long corridor where a dozen children were propped
up on pillows in their beds. The delight in their eyes
made her forget her own troubles for the moment.

"These are the children most in need of hope,"
Chester whispered to her. "Promise them anything
they want that doesn't need feeding. No puppies or
kittens, I'm afraid. Against orphanage rules."

"I know," Sylvie said, and then wished she
hadn't. Chester's gaze seemed to pin her.

"Being alone at Christmas is one of the worst
things that can happen," he said. "But these children
aren't alone. The staff here at St. Mary's cares a great
deal what happens to them."

"But staff can never be a parent," Sylvie said,
fighting the lump in her throat.

"Sometimes a place like this is better than a home
without love," Chester said. He put a hand on her
shoulder. "From what I've seen of life, it isn't so
difficult surviving a childhood without love. The hard
thing is learning, as an adult, that you deserve love,"
he said, bending low to her ear. "Is that what you'd
like for Christmas...someone to love?"

Sylvie wanted to pull away from him, but he

meant only kindness. And why was she acting like a maudlin fool? She'd survived the orphanage, the streets and the adolescent dangers of a city that ate young girls like peanuts. She looked down the room at the expectant faces. The sheets were immaculately white, the children's hair combed. It was obvious they were well cared for. They were among the lucky.

As was she.

She walked past Chester to the first bed and sat lightly on the edge. "What can Santa bring you?" she asked, smiling down at the child.

They slowly made their way around the room, taking a moment with each youngster. Sylvie obediently wrote down each wish, wondering why Chester bothered when he'd already brought the presents he intended to give. But the process seemed to delight the children, and she watched with a strange happiness as Chester did his work.

When they were finished, Chester stopped her at the door. "What do you really know about Dr. Semmes?" he asked.

Sylvie was taken aback. Chester had only been kind to her, but he seemed to have moved to a more parental role. And though she wanted his opinion of Hunter Semmes, she was also a little uneasy. "He's a doctor and a toy maker," she said carefully.

"Nothing more?" he asked.

Sylvie didn't have time to answer before the door opened and Alice poked her head in. "We have to leave, Sylvie. We're going to be late. Dr. Semmes has offered us a ride to the store, but we're still pushing it."

Sylvie didn't have to check her watch. Alice was

always dead-on about time. She turned to the older man. "It was a delightful lunch," she said, taking his hand. "Thanks for asking me."

Chester's gaze was on Alice. "I'll be in touch," he said, a puzzled tone in his voice. "I have several other stops this season. I might call on you to help again."

"Of course," Sylvie said.

"It was a pleasure meeting you, Alice McBride," Chester said, lifting Alice's hand for a kiss that sent her into giggles.

When Sylvie started to leave, she felt Chester's hand.

"The list," he whispered. "I need it."

Sylvie gave him the pad and then hurried after Alice, who was walking away awfully fast.

"Where's the fire?" Sylvie asked as she drew abreast of her friend.

"As if you didn't know," Alice said, but there was a giggle in her voice.

They joined Hunter, who looked at both women with a question.

"This one here is a vixen," Alice said, pointing at Sylvie and winking at Hunter. "You watch out for her, my fine young man. She sings one song and dances to another."

Sylvie saw the doubt in his eyes and thought to tell him what Alice was talking about. Sylvie couldn't deny that she was hoping to start a friendship between Alice and Chester—and it looked as if she might have been successful. But she didn't want Hunter to get the idea that she was in the business of playing matchmaker. Especially since she couldn't look at him without feeling warmth flush over her body.

"The car is in the side lot," Hunter said as he allowed Alice to lead the way. His touch on Sylvie's arm made her both hot and cold. "We need to talk," he said to her in a lower voice.

During the ride to the store, Alice kept up a steady chatter about her grandchildren and the cookies, cakes, pies and candy she was preparing for the on-slaught of holiday visiting.

Sitting beside Hunter, Sylvie contributed little to the conversation, but she couldn't keep her gaze from straying across the car to Hunter's face, his hands on the wheel. Capable hands. If only he would reach across and touch her…but he didn't.

Sylvie knew that part of his reticence came from her own behavior. She sat stiffly in her seat, unwilling to show her feelings in front of Alice. It was too risky. It put her in too vulnerable a position. If Hunter stepped out of her life as quickly as he'd stepped in, she didn't want Alice feeling sorry for her.

Pity was the worst of all emotions. She knew from personal experience that once pity took root, it left no room for any other emotions. Pity killed pride and love and compassion.

She'd felt pity when she first stepped into the or-phanage. But Chester Fenton had pushed it away. He'd made her see that the children didn't pity them-selves, and therefore she had no right to pity them. It was something she'd have to think long and hard about in regard to her own past.

Hunter pulled into the back of the store as Sylvie directed him. Alice sprang from the back seat like a teenager, thanking Hunter and rolling her eyes at Sylvie before she hurried inside.

Sylvie looked at Hunter and hoped she was concealing her thoughts. She had flashes of him, asleep or just waking. Tiny split seconds of pleasure that darted through her mind like wicked forks of lightning. It was horribly distracting, and she had no desire to reveal the depth of her foolishness to him.

"I got the two Mollys," Hunter said. "It's just the Buster left out there, as far as I can tell."

"You haven't heard from the…opposition?" Sylvie wasn't certain what to call the enemy.

"Nothing." Hunter drummed his fingers on the steering wheel. "I keep having these terrible images of some child with that doll—" He broke off.

"We'll get it back," Sylvie said reaching across the car and touching his shoulder. She did it without thinking, but once she touched the fabric of his jacket, felt the lean muscle beneath, she knew it was not an innocent touch. Nothing about her feelings for Hunter was innocent. She forced herself to concentrate on the problem at hand. "Do you have any idea who might be behind this?"

He turned his head abruptly to look at her. "You think it's someone I know?"

Sylvie bit her bottom lip. "I wouldn't want to think that, but it's possible. I mean, how long had the dolls been on the market before this happened?" She found that her mind was suddenly clear on several important points.

Before he could answer, she had another question. "Hunter, did anything strange happen before this? I mean any break-in attempts, odd visitors, anything at all? I think this whole process started months back."

He looked at her with amazement and then admiration. "Nothing that stands out in my mind, but then that's exactly the way it would have been planned. I'll have to think about those questions. You've got a good head on your shoulders, Sylvie West."

"And I'm going to be fired if I don't go inside." She wanted him to kiss her—to reassure her that the night they'd spent together was still in his mind. She wanted to reach out and touch his face, and it occurred to her for the first time that perhaps he needed some indication of her feelings. That he might not trust his own.

She was about to touch his cheek when she saw him lean toward her. His kiss was a whisper of sensual pleasure along her cheek.

"Can I pick you up after work?" he asked.

Sylvie felt her heart pounding so hard she thought she might not be able to speak. "Only if you bring Familiar," she said, her voice a hoarse whisper.

"I'm glad to see you think we need a chaperon," he answered.

"Oh, we need a chaperon," she said, fighting a rush of desire. "We definitely need someone to watch over us."

"See you at seven," Hunter said. "I'll be parked right here."

SYLVIE'S MIND WAS ON everything except her work. She felt Alice's elbow in her ribs and looked up to see a handsome woman eyeing her with a mixture of impatience and amusement.

"If it doesn't intrude too much on your daydreaming, I'd like to make a purchase," the woman said.

"Of course." Sylvie reached for the toys the woman held. "I'm afraid my mind wandered."

"Christmas is a great time of year for fantasies," the woman said. "The only trouble is that all too often reality doesn't live up to fantasy."

"Now that's not the attitude to have at Christmas," Alice interjected. "This is the time of year when anything is possible. Miracles happen, you know."

"Only in Bible stories and movies," the woman said, then laughed. "I've become something of a cynic, I'm afraid."

"I know the type," Alice said, giving Sylvie a knowing look. "But it's a question of what comes first, the miracle or the belief. Since no one can prove which, I always take the safer route and believe in miracles."

The woman laughed and handed over her credit card. Sylvie felt as if she'd been punched in the stomach. The name on the card was Connie Semmes. She looked up into the brown-eyed gaze of the woman and knew instantly that this was, indeed, Hunter's ex-wife.

To prove the point, the woman looked her square in the eye. "Miss West, may I have a word with you?" Connie Semmes said as she took her sack of toys.

Sylvie gave Alice a helpless look.

"I'll cover the counter, but don't be long," Alice offered.

Sylvie followed Connie Semmes to a section of the store that was almost quiet.

"I spoke with Hunter," Connie said quickly. "He used me as an alibi to bail him out of being a suspect in the toy theft. I didn't press him for the truth on whether or not he was that crazy Santa. I didn't want to know. Anyway, he mentioned your name. I just wanted to stop by and tell you that he's a great guy. One of the best. Just don't rely on him." Her gaze was level. "Don't follow him down the yellow brick road." She sighed. "I'm not trying to be negative. It's just that Hunter has always been…he gets so involved with those damn toys that he's like a child."

Sylvie said nothing. She watched Connie's face carefully. She saw a hint of anger, frustration and concern. "Why are you telling me this?" she finally asked.

"Hunter is one of the best people I've ever known. But he lives in a dream world." She shrugged and turned away. "I'm sorry, this was a mistake."

"You're still in love with Hunter, aren't you?" Sylvie asked, feeling dizzy.

Connie turned around, a sheaf of auburn hair swinging across her face. "No. I gave up loving Hunter a long time ago. I've found the man I want to marry. But I care what happens to Hunter. I want him to get professional help. And I know this is desperate, but if you have any influence on him, please ask him to see someone."

"Why are you telling *me* this?" Sylvie asked again, this time with a different emphasis.

"I heard Hunter's voice, the way he spoke of you. Help him." She shook her head again. "This was foolish of me. I was in the store shopping with a little friend of mine and I thought I'd give it a shot. Good luck, Miss West."

Before Sylvie could respond, Connie was gone,

her sack of toys clutched in her hand and her high
heels clicking over the floor.

HUNTER WENT TO ANSWER the door with the hope
that somehow Sylvie had gotten off work and decided to surprise him. She was one of the most con-
fusing women he'd ever met. They'd shared a night
together—a night of passion and tenderness. And yet
the next day he felt as if he'd slept with someone
who looked like her.

He knew from his own reaction that the barrier
she erected was more than likely a safety device to
protect her from being hurt. It was the same reaction
he had. Together, they could learn not to put up the
protective wall. But first they were going to have to
learn how to talk, openly.

And as important as that was, Hunter also knew
that solving the mystery of what was happening with
his dolls was the top priority. If Sylvie didn't understand that, then they really had no future together,
anyway.

His thoughts were on Sylvie and his dolls when
he opened the door. To his surprise, Lila Vernon
stood there, still in her nurse's uniform.

"You're one hard man to find," the pretty blonde
said, holding out a manila folder. "I couldn't get the
original test results, so I ran you a copy. I hope that's
good enough."

Hunter wanted to hug the nurse. "Lila, you are the
best," he said, ushering her into his shop. He wanted
to tear open the envelope, but he also wanted to let
the woman know how much he appreciated her ef-
forts.

"How are the Wescott children?"

"They're going home tomorrow," she said. "In plenty of time to enjoy Christmas."

Hunter felt immense relief. "What did the tests show?" He held the envelope, but he knew Lila could sum it up fast.

"Nothing much, that I could tell." The nurse frowned. "Nothing showed up as toxic, but there were some strange enzymes that were isolated. It was almost as if someone deliberately gave them something that would make them violently ill, then clear out of their systems fast. Those two kids act as if they'd never been sick for a moment. And they were so sick."

Hunter nodded. He was delighted the children were well. But he was troubled by the inability of the hospital to pinpoint exactly what had made them sick.

"You go over the reports and see if you can find something," Lila said. "I looked for the expected things. I'm sure there's information there that you can get a lot more out of than I did."

"I owe you a big favor," Hunter said. He did. She'd gone out of her way to help him. She had also broken a few hospital rules and risked her job.

"How about you come back to work at the hospital. Even as a volunteer one day a week. There are children who need medical attention."

Hunter considered it. "Maybe after the first of the year," he said.

"After the holidays," she agreed. She looked past him into the toy shop. "I'd love a tour," she said. "It isn't every day that a medical doctor gives up a lucrative practice to carve wooden spindles and make dolls."

Hunter smiled. "You want the nickel tour or the dime tour?"

"Whatever you have time for."

Hunter took her through the ground floor, showing the toys he'd made but being very careful not to mention the Molly or Buster dolls.

"Do you have a toy for this year's Christmas?" she asked. "Isn't that when the major toy makers market their new products?"

Hunter raised an eyebrow. "I didn't realize you were interested in the business of toy making?"

"I'm not. It just seems that it would be a good idea. It is the season for children, gifts, all of those things that make a consumer's heart go pitter-pat. And I did have another motive."

Hunter felt a small chill. "What might that be?"

"I was hoping to get an exclusive toy for my niece and nephew. They're a little bored by the doctor kits and the new underwear."

Hunter laughed out loud. He was becoming as cynical as Sylvie, and it felt good to be proven wrong. "I do have a couple of wooden house kits that I'm thinking about marketing. How about those? They're prototypes and not available yet, but I feel that in the next few years they might be something every child wants to own." He found the kits and brought her two.

"You mean you'd let me have them now?" Lila leaned up and kissed his cheek. "You're too generous, Hunter." She looked into his eyes. "I know this is forward, but I have to ask. Are you available?"

For a moment he didn't catch her meaning, and when he did, he shook his head. "It's very flattering that you ask, Lila. But—"

She touched his lips with her fingers. "I'm sorry," she said. "I shouldn't have asked that." She turned away and walked to the door. "You're a good man, Hunter. I just want you to know that."

Hunter watched as she let herself out of the toy shop and quietly closed the door. It was only after she was gone that he noticed the manila envelope that had obviously been pushed under the door. He picked it up and tore open the flap.

Chapter Nine

Hunter unfolded the single sheet of white typing paper and looked at the typewritten words.

On Christmas Day a child will die because of your doll. It will be a long and painful death. You can prevent this. Give us the formula and a legal document saying you will make no claim to it. At 10:00 p.m. be at The Jungle Room bar on Forty-second Street. There will be a package behind the bar with more instructions.

Hunter read the note three times before he put it down. Anger boiled inside him. The idea that a child, an innocent toddler, was in jeopardy as part of a blackmail scheme, infuriated him. He'd always abhorred violence, but he knew at that moment that if he had the culprits in front of him, he'd take great pleasure in hurting them.

He couldn't allow himself the luxury of fury. He'd known the doll was out there, a time bomb waiting to go off. And he also knew that it was up to him to find the doll and retrieve it before another child was injured.

It wasn't his fault that the doll had been contaminated. The note was solid proof that someone had done something to Buster Bigboy. He could take the note to the authorities and finally prove to them that he wasn't some kind of kook. The process of the law was so slow, though, that a child might die before anything was done. And although he had the note, he had no way to prove he hadn't written it himself.

Though he was hamstrung with the authorities, that didn't relieve him of his responsibility. He'd created the dolls, touted them as a breakthrough in child health. And some unsuspecting parent had taken him at his word, bought the doll, and now had it waiting under a Christmas tree. The doll embodied the expectation of a Christmas morning of surprise and joy. Instead, there would be pain and suffering, a rushed trip to the hospital emergency room and, finally, tragedy.

His heart pounded with renewed anger. Who could do such a thing? Who could use a child as a bargaining chip in a game of greed? When he found out, he was going to make them pay.

Until then, he had to play along. If it were only a matter of money, he'd give them the formula without a fight. But there was so much more than money at stake. The dolls could save poor children from disease.

And he wasn't going to give that up.

He felt a sudden rubbing against his leg and looked down to find the black cat winding through his legs.

"We can figure this out, can't we?" he asked, scooping the cat into his arms.

"Meow," Familiar said, nipping his chin lightly. "Meow."

SO, THE BAD GUYS have ratcheted up the heat a bit. Hunter looks as if he could spit nails he's so angry. But the truth is, the blackmail note is a good thing. From my experience as an incredibly successful private investigator, the forces of good must wait until the opposition makes a move. At this point in the game, we can only counter whatever they do. But each time they move, it gives us clues to figure out who they are.

Take, for instance, this little note. Hunter is a doctor and inventor, with a healthy dose of the do-gooder. An interesting combination of qualities. It's rare to meet someone who honestly wants to make the world a better place. Most humanoids, motivated as they are by appetite, want to make their individual lives better. This is the quality that has made them the dominant species. Hunter is no martyr. But he is that rare human who has looked past his own horizon.

In reading the note, he has visualized the agony of a poisoned child. Nothing more. What he's missed is the way the note is written. It starts out 'On Christmas Day.' A telling phrase. This entire scenario has been deliberately constructed. It's true that the good doctor has launched his dolls at the Christmas season, but there's something more there. The author of the note is educated, not one of the thugs we dispatched so nicely in KATZ Meow.

This is a person who uses words carefully. The ordinary blackmail note is brief, harsh, even. This note takes the time to point blame, to saddle the good *doctor with the end results, should he choose not to play nice.*

All very interesting.

As far as the physical preparation of the note, it was written on a computer or word processor and printed out with a laser printer. High-quality print. Not a fancy script. Someone who goes for clarity rather than style.

I must cogitate over these factors. I'm getting a picture of the human behind this scheme. Not exactly the image one wants to hold dear during the season of Madonna and Child. But it's a clue that can't be ignored. Now I think I saw some more of that sirloin in the fridge. I'll see how smart our inventor friend actually is—if I can make him understand that a little ground meat sautéed with garlic and a pinch of that fresh dill in his window would certainly speed my brain function.

THE BLAST OF WIND WAS COLD as Sylvie walked out of KATZ Meow Toy Emporium. She immediately spotted Hunter's car and felt her heart begin to race. Would she always feel such a rush of anticipation and pleasure at the sight of him? It was a question she wasn't sure she wanted answered. For once, she didn't want to kill the feeling with cynicism and hard reality.

He must have seen her smile, because he opened his door, got out and started walking briskly toward her. His arms circled her and pulled her into a hug, and she let his warmth surround her.

"It's good to see you," he said.

"It's good to feel you," she answered, laughing. She wasn't the flirtatious or light-hearted kind, but

Hunter made her feel as if she were. "Where's the cat? I can't go with you unless he's here to chaperon," she teased.

"Familiar." Hunter pointed to the car where the cat was perched in the back window. "He insisted on coming—after making me cook a meal."

It wasn't until Sylvie backed away from him that she saw the tension in his eyes, the hard set of his mouth.

"What's wrong?" she asked.

"A lot, but it's better since you're here." He opened the passenger door and seated her before he walked around and got in himself.

"Did something happen?" Sylvie asked when he put the car in drive and took off.

"I have an appointment tonight. I'm supposed to pick up instructions on how to hand over my formula for the dolls. In a bar called The Jungle Room."

Sylvie tried to control her reaction, but she couldn't completely. She'd once worked as a bartender there. It hadn't been a good time in her life.

"What is it?" Hunter asked.

Sylvie remembered what the thin man had said to her. Would her background make a difference to Hunter? They were worlds apart. Maybe even solar systems. A week ago she would have insisted that two such different people could never have cared for each other. Now she wasn't so sure. But it was time to put it to the test.

"I know that place," she said. "It's dark, and a lot of people drift in and out. The regulars are okay, but…"

"A perfect point of rendezvous for someone with dirty business."

She nodded. "It would be. But—" She turned in the seat so she could watch his face. "It also gives us a slight advantage. Joey Monk owns that bar. I've known him most of my life. He might be able to help us out here."

"As in keeping an eye open for whoever delivers the package?"

"That, and maybe giving me a rundown on the two men who attacked us last night in the store. I think I could describe them." The smile that touched his face made her blood rush. In the world she'd grown up in, people didn't show emotion. Not sorrow or joy. To know a man who was secure enough to show his feelings was almost a miracle in itself.

"I'll drive you over there."

She thought for a few seconds. "No, I think I should go alone. The type of people..." She broke off. "Joey knows me. I think he would be honest with me."

"But not with me?" Hunter asked.

Sylvie hadn't chosen the moment. It had come without invitation. "I grew up pretty rough. You should know that. If it bothers you, we might as well get it out in the open now. Joey and his friends were the kids in my neighborhood." She watched his face carefully but saw no sign of pity or contempt or any of the emotions she couldn't bear.

"We all grew up hard, just in different ways," he said. "You're who you are because of your background, Sylvie, and don't ever doubt that I believe you're one hell of a woman."

She felt the smile grow on her face, and she knew without looking in the mirror that he could see her happiness as clearly as if she'd written the word on her forehead.

Maybe it wasn't too late for her to learn to be open with her feelings, too. Maybe miracles did happen.

SYLVIE PULLED HER JACKET closer around her and leaned her elbows on the bar. The Jungle Room hadn't changed much, except the patrons seemed older. "Been a long time, Joey," she said.

"Yeah," Joey Monk answered as he studied Sylvie. "You look different."

"How so?" Sylvie asked. "Maybe a few years older?" she said with a grin.

"That…" Monk narrowed his eyes. "But something else. You've lost your edge."

Sylvie took a deep breath. "Maybe a little. I'd like to lose a lot more."

Monk threw the dish towel over his shoulder and came toward her. Before she asked, he poured up a measure of bourbon and dropped ice cubes in it. He pushed the drink across the bar to her. "Have one on me for old time's sake. I haven't had a barkeep with your kind of speed since you left. What were you then, all of eighteen?"

Sylvie picked up the glass and sipped. She felt him watching her. She had been just eighteen and finally figuring out that life with Augie was not what she wanted. It had been a bad time for her, and Joey had been a loyal friend.

"I haven't grown horns, have I?" she asked.

"I'd have to look closer." Joey cocked his head. "I'm not a man who believes in coincidence, so I find it very strange that Augie Marcel was in here two days ago bringing up your name."

Sylvie almost choked on the tiny amount of bourbon she was about to swallow.

"Augie? What was he doing here?"

"He *said* he was in the neighborhood and stopped by for a drink. He asked if I'd seen you. I thought it was all over between the two of you."

The disapproval in Joey's tone was hard to miss.

"It's been over. I haven't seen Augie in better than ten years." Long over, and Sylvie never liked to remember the days when she'd been involved with the man.

"Strange he should reappear, and now you."

"More than strange." Sylvie tried not to show the depth of her concern. "But that's Augie. He turns up where you least expect him."

"I thought you moved away," Monk said, leaning one hand on the polished bar.

"I did. But I came back." She finally met his gaze. "I got a job in a toy store." Even she couldn't stop her smile.

"I thought you hated Christmas and kids and all of that." Joey arched his eyebrows. "I remember when—" He halted abruptly.

"You remember when Ken and Kevin died. I remember, too." She didn't look away from him. The past was almost tangible, there in the hard memories they both shared.

"You almost broke my heart," Joey said softly.

"I know," she said. "You were all of fourteen and I was twelve. You looked out for me, a lot better than my mom."

Joey reached across the bar and patted Sylvie's arm. "You were like my sister. When they took you away, it was like my own family. So how was St. Mary's?''

''Not so bad.'' To her surprise, Sylvie found that the memories that sprang to mind were not bad ones. ''We ate and went to school. The nuns were pretty frightening, at first. But I did well in class. They liked me.''

He motioned to her drink. ''Knock that back and tell me what brings you to my bar. I know this isn't a trip down memory lane.''

Sylvie took another sip of the drink. ''I do need help.'' She sighed as she tried to figure out how much to tell Joey. He'd always been square with her, but even as a young boy, he'd been working the rackets. And this bar was the pickup place. She had to be very, very careful.

''Has anybody left a package at the bar?'' she asked.

''For you?'' Joey's dark eyebrows rose again. ''Who would know you'd be coming in here today?''

''Not for me. For Hunter Semmes.''

''Hunter.'' Joey said the name slowly. ''Not from our neighborhood, huh?''

''He's a doctor,'' Sylvie said, knowing that Joey's suspicion of someone with wealth would be instantaneous. ''A pediatrician. It's a long story, but if I had to put my life on it, I'd say he was one of the good guys, Joey.''

''I don't believe in good guys,'' the bartender said, easing back away from the bar a distance of two feet. He bent down and checked under it. ''No package.''

Sylvie could tell by the stiff way he held his shoulders that she'd upset him. He viewed her as a traitor, another of the women who'd hooked up with a man with money. One of the girls who'd used her looks to barter a better life. It was the daydream of many a poor girl who saw no other route of escape.

"He's a good guy," Sylvie repeated softly. "And he could be in a lot of trouble."

"And this should matter to me?" Joey turned away from her.

"I told him I knew you, that maybe you would help."

"You spoke out of turn, Sylvie."

"I don't think I did."

He faced her again. "You're gone for years and then you come back in here and tell me what I should do—that's not how it works around this neighborhood."

"I remember how it works, Joey. You're the one who sat with me at the funeral home with my dead brothers. I remember exactly how it works. This man, this doctor, is trying to do something good. He doesn't deserve what's happening to him."

"I should care? You're making my eyes tear up."

Sylvie slid off the barstool. "Time has changed you, too, Joey. It's made you a real jackass." She turned to leave knowing that her one chance to really help Hunter had disappeared.

She pushed the door open, and the dark night seemed to settle over her as she stepped out. She was surprised at the lightness of Joey's touch as he caught her shoulder and turned her around as he simultaneously drew her back inside. "What do you want me to do?" he asked.

"Let me describe some men to you. Tell me if you remember them."

"Remember? You think they're from the old neighborhood?"

Sylvie lifted shoulder. "One of them seemed to know me. A tall man, very thin. Blond hair, thinning. Fondness for black clothes." She smiled slightly. "It sounds melodramatic, I know, but he's strong for his build. About forty, maybe. Icy eyes." She thought she saw a flicker cross Joey's face, but he didn't say anything.

"The other guy is harder. Big, strong, ordinary face, brown hair and eyes."

"Like any Joe on the street."

"Unfortunately, that's about the truth. But the thin man, there was something in his eyes. He's smart. I think if you met him, you'd remember him."

Joey looked toward the bar where a patron lifted a glass in a signal for a refill. "I'll think about it. If someone comes to mind, I'll let you know. And I'll ask around."

Sylvie put her hand on his shoulder. "People don't often change, Joey. You've always been someone I could count on."

"What about the package?" he asked, waving at the patron that he was on the way.

"Keep an eye on the bar. See who leaves a package. Call me at this number as soon as someone does. I'll be outside and I'm going to follow him." She handed him a slip of paper.

Joey's eyes narrowed. "That doesn't sound smart. In fact, it sounds downright dangerous."

"I know what I'm doing."

For the first time in a while the corners of his mouth turned up. "Now that's the old Sylvie. Determined and with just enough sass to stare down anyone who dared to cross her.''

"I'm mostly the same, but I think I have changed a little, Joey. I want to be able to hope, to think maybe there are good things and good people out there. For a long time I was afraid to even try to believe. I didn't want to be hurt.'' She leaned up and kissed his cheek. "I'm not as afraid anymore.''

"If this guy has done this for you, he must be okay,'' Joey said slowly. He took the piece of paper she handed him and looked at the phone number. "You got some backup?'' he asked.

Sylvie nodded and made sure she didn't flinch as she looked into his eyes. "I've got backup and I'll be fine.''

HUNTER KNOCKED for the fifth time in less than an hour on Sylvie's door. She'd promised to be ready. He checked his watch and pounded again. Finally the door opened and the older woman he recognized as Alice looked out at him.

"She's gone,'' Alice said.

"Where?'' Hunter felt a tremor of foreboding.

"She wouldn't say. She just told me to wait by the phone and not to answer the door until nine-thirty and then to tell you she'd gone.''

Hunter knew then—she'd stayed at the bar to stalk the deliveryman. "Alice,'' he said, reaching into the door and gently grasping the older woman's shoulder. "What time did she leave?''

"About eight o'clock,'' Alice said. Her brow furrowed. "She's up to something, isn't she?''

"I'm afraid she is.''

"Is she in danger?" Alice's keen blue eyes narrowed. "That girl is as headstrong as a bull."

"You can say that again." Hunter started down the hallway of the older apartment building. He was at the stairs when he heard Alice call out.

"Wait up for me," she said.

"Alice, this could be—"

"Dangerous? You nitwit, that's why I'm coming. If something goes wrong, you'll need someone who's calm in an emergency. That's me. And if anyone hurts Sylvie, they're going to have to go through me first."

Chapter Ten

The cell phone she'd rented chirped against her hip-bone and Sylvie snatched it up, flipping it open. "Yes?"

"There's a guy at the bar. He looks like the second man you described. He has a manila envelope. He could be your target."

Sylvie closed her eyes briefly. Now that the moment had come, she was afraid. "Thanks, Joey."

"I don't like this, Sylvie. Where are you?"

"Right outside. All I'm going to do is follow him. Sort of turn the tables for a change."

"These guys aren't dumb," Joey warned her. "This is what they do for a living. If he catches on to the fact that you're tailing him, he might lead you right into trouble."

For a split second, Sylvie was reminded of the old days, back when Joey taught her how to survive in a neighborhood that showed no mercy for the weak or stupid.

"I remember," she said. "I won't go into any dark alleys, no heroics."

"I wish I believed you. So what about the envelope?"

"Give it to Hunter when he comes. Just give him a chance." She spoke the last softly. It was odd, but even though they hadn't seen each other in years, Sylvie felt almost as if Joey were her family. She wanted his approval. Especially of Hunter.

"I'll look him over."

"I know you will," she said.

"He's coming out now," Joey whispered urgently.

"Thanks." She snapped the phone shut and tapped the cab driver on the shoulder. When the door of the bar opened and the man she recognized as one of her would-be abductors came out, she pointed to him. "Follow that man. Don't lose him. There's a big tip in it for you."

The driver glanced over his shoulder and lifted an eyebrow. "Is somebody filming a movie and forgot to tell me?"

"Yeah, and you're the star," Sylvie said.

The cabby gunned the motor. "Great, but I want to talk to the script writer. The dialogue is terrible. You sound like something from the seventies."

Sylvie gripped the back of the front seat. "That's what I love about New York. Everyone's a critic." But she knew she'd hopped the right cab when the driver whipped through the traffic in pursuit of the quarry. This was a man who knew how to drive.

NOW ISN'T THAT JUST like a headstrong sprite—to rush off into the teeth of danger. She's gone off thinking she can handle this all on her own. Not accurate. But I admire the overtones of feline empowerment. I can't say that to Dr. Inventor. He's about to have a panic attack. And he's driving like the proverbial bat out of hell. An interesting way with language, these humans have. Who would think of a bat in hell, and then visualize it fleeing? For a lower life form, humanoids do have some interesting moments.

Oh, no! We almost didn't make that corner. I think Alice must have gained a few more white hairs. But she's taking charge, talking calmly to Hunter and getting him to slow down. The voice of reason— thank goodness for Alice.

And what a woman! She managed to snatch up a bag of homemade macadamia-nut, chocolate-chip cookies. I've eaten two, and the rest of the bag is in jeopardy! There's nothing like a rush of chocolate to go with danger.

Here we are at the bar. The Jungle Room. Dig the neon palm tree with the monkey swinging back and forth in the branches. Reminds me of some of the great neon of the fifties. Now this is a place with atmosphere. I hate to say it, but I'll fit in a lot better in this place than Alice.

Luckily, I think Hunter is going to impress on her the need to stay out of the bar.

A quick check of the dash shows it's fifteen minutes until show time. I'd like to get in there first and scope things out—I only wish Sylvie had thought to take me with her. That impulsive creature.

I have the feeling that she's around here some-where, but I don't dare leave Dr. Claus. Between the two of them, I credit Sylvie with the most sense and ability to survive. Except for that tiny little streak of impulsiveness. When this is all over, I think I'll have to make an appointment for her with a behaviorist. A few rubber bands snapping on her wrist with each impulsive thought should break this nasty habit. Human training is very much like that of training a canine. Persistence and patience are the key words.

Better make my move for the door. I can only imagine what Dr. Claus will do in a place like The Jungle Room.

AS SOON AS HE WALKED in the door, Hunter knew he was too late. He also knew that Sylvie had been there, and that she was well-known to the big, burly man behind the bar.

He ordered a drink and took a seat. When he felt a light touch against his legs, he knew Familiar was with him. He had a healthy skepticism about the cat and the detective agency, but with each passing incident, he'd begun to believe that Familiar was an extraordinary animal.

The bartender put his drink down and leaned over. "If you're Hunter Semmes, I have something for you."

"I am," Hunter said. He didn't have to ask how the man had identified him. He was obviously a fish out of water.

The bartender brought a manila envelope out from under the bar and handed it over. As Hunter took it, the bartender kept a grip on it.

"I've got a special fondness for Sylvie West," the man said. "I hope you're not involving her in anything dangerous."

"I hope not, too," Hunter said.

The man released the envelope. "The guy who left it was a stranger. Tell that to Sylvie when you see her."

"Do you know where she is?" Hunter asked.

The man looked slightly startled. "She's following him. Didn't she tell you?"

Hunter's stomach knotted. "No." He stood up immediately. "She didn't tell me that. But I should have known." He'd figured she'd gone to the bar and stayed to see who made the delivery, but he honestly hadn't considered that she would do something so dangerous as attempting to follow one of the blackmailers.

Joey's olive complexion paled. "I don't like this," he said. He leaned closer. "What's this all about?"

Hunter hesitated. "I have something these men want."

"Something you want more than Sylvie?"

Hunter hadn't framed the question in exactly that fashion. "There's a lot more at stake here than one person."

"From where I'm sitting, there's only one person. Sylvie. You let anything happen to her—"

"Innocent children could die," Hunter said grimly. "Keep that in mind. I know this is as important to Sylvie as it is to me." He picked up the envelope and started out of the bar.

"Hey," Joey said. He motioned him back. "Check out a guy named Augie Marcel."

Hunter's neck tingled. "Who is that?"

"Someone from Sylvie's past. Someone bad." He cut his eyes to the corner of the room. "Do you know that dame?"

Hunter hadn't noticed the woman sitting alone at a dark table. She was shadowed and her face was concealed by a windswept hairdo and cigarette smoke. She was staring at the men at the bar.

"Never seen her." Hunter stepped away. Sylvie was out in the city trailing blackmailers. He didn't have time for foolishness.

"I'm asking for a reason," Joey said. "She's

never been in here. This isn't a bar that attracts a lot
of tourist trade. Make it a point to walk by her," he
said.

Hunter felt the tug of impatience, but he nodded.
"I'll go to the men's room." He started across the
bar, pretending to stumble on a chair leg near the
woman's table. He caught himself on the chair in
front of her and offered an apology.

He knew instantly that Joey's tip had been a good
one. The woman turned away, grabbing her purse,
but not before Hunter saw the rock on her hand. It
was a large diamond. Not the kind of jewelry one
would wear in a downtown bar. He was fairly certain,
too, that the red hair that swung over her cheekbones
was a wig. He was tempted to make a snatch for it,
but he restrained the impulse.

He mumbled another apology and hurried into the
men's room. The woman was as out of place in the
bar as he was, but that didn't automatically link her
to the blackmailing scheme. On the other hand she
was the only lead he had at the moment. Sylvie was
out there—possibly in grave danger. And he didn't
have a clue where she might be.

He opened the envelope. Inside was a Polaroid
snapshot of a young boy, a toddler of about two. He
held the package of a Buster Bigboy and stared into
the camera with a smile.

Hunter's stomach knotted at the idea that the child
was in danger. The blackmailers had put a personal
face on the scheme. That it was a deliberate effort to
manipulate him was clear, and it also didn't matter.

There was only a brief note attached. It read, "You
can follow directions. Go home, prepare the docu-

mentation for the formula and the patent. We'll be in touch."

Hunter clenched his hand into a fist, wanting to lash out at anyone. Instead, he hurried from the bathroom. The table where the woman had sat was empty.

The bartender pointed to the doorway, and Hunter took off. When he stepped into the night, he saw only the flow of traffic. Then Familiar stepped out of the shadows.

"Meow!" The cat ran toward him and then on to the car. Hunter followed, disgusted that he'd let the woman slip away from him.

On the one hand he had instructions to go home. On the other, he had to try and find Sylvie. He opened the car door to find Alice pointing at a green sedan pulling out of a lot. As Familiar leaped in beside him, Alice said, "That woman came out of the bar at a run! Is she involved?"

Hunter didn't bother to answer, he started the car and took off in hot pursuit.

"The cat followed her, so I knew she had to be important," Alice explained as they wove through the busy traffic, the taillights of the sedan always in front of them.

"Thank goodness for you and Familiar," Hunter said, his attention focused on the traffic. He still had the woman's taillights clearly in view.

"Where's Sylvie?" Alice asked.

"I hope we're going to find out," Hunter said as he made a right-hand turn.

SYLVIE STOOD IN THE SHADOWS outside the building, wondering why she'd thought it would be a good idea to tail anyone. The man had driven straight to the office building and disappeared inside. She'd been there for half an hour and knew nothing more than she had when she first arrived.

The waiting was beginning to chafe at her, but she wasn't certain what to do next. She dialed Hunter's number and listened to the phone ring. Why didn't he have an answering machine? She knew he'd be worried about her. She was supposed to be helping him. He probably thought she'd backed out on him.

Her mind churned with thoughts and worries as she ticked off the minutes. She'd give it another ten, and then she would go on to Hunter's. Even as she thought it, she looked for a cab to hail. This was the business district, and so late at night, not many cabbies were looking for fares. But there was always the bus or the subway.

Footsteps echoed on the pavement, and she ducked as tightly against the building as she could. Someone was walking toward her! She'd been so intent on watching the building that she hadn't paid any attention to what was happening behind her.

The only thing she could do was try to melt against the limestone of the wall. She could feel her heart pounding, pounding, and her lungs felt as if they were on fire, but she was too afraid to breathe.

The man was so close she could hear the regular intake of his breath as she tried to make herself invisible.

He passed right by her, headed for the same door the man she'd tailed had taken. At the door, the man paused.

In the glare of the streetlight, Sylvie saw his features. For a moment she didn't believe her eyes. It wasn't possible. It simply couldn't be.

Augie Marcel grasped the door handle and stepped into the building.

Sylvie hadn't really believed Joey when he'd said Augie had been in the bar. She hadn't accepted the emotional impact of it. Now she had to accept it, and she was left trembling against the stone wall, too stunned to even begin to try to put the pieces of the puzzle together.

THE GREEN SEDAN STOPPED at the guardhouse of the exclusive neighborhood. Hunter had no choice but to drive by, but he went as slowly as he could without drawing attention.

"The guard is bending down and talking to her," Alice said, doing her best to see everything, as Hunter concentrated on the driving. "That's some neighborhood."

Hunter knew the area. It was pretty ritzy for a patron of The Jungle Room.

"She's going in," Alice said. "She either lives there or she knows the right thing to say. They wouldn't let us in there on a bet." Alice pulled a pen and a scrap of paper from her purse and paused. "Her tag is covered with mud," she said in a shocked tone. "She lives in a place like that and there's mud on her tag!"

Hunter looked over at Alice. "It sounds like someone deliberately obstructed the numbers." He nodded approval. "And it also sounds like you've done this before."

"Common sense," Alice said, waving her hand.

"That's all we're going to get here. Now let's find Sylvie. I'm worried sick about that girl."

"I wish I knew how to find her," Hunter said, once again swept by a feeling of foreboding. "She could be in danger."

"Meow!" Familiar cried.

"Maybe we should go to your place and wait for her," Alice suggested. "She won't let you down, Hunter. Maybe she's discovered something important. Once that girl puts her mind to something, she won't let go."

Hunter smiled. Alice was correct—and it was one of the things he loved about Sylvie. Even as he thought it, he realized the significance of it. He didn't just like her, he was falling in love with her. Deeply.

"Quit grinning like a hound with a basted turkey on Thanksgiving and get us to your place," Alice said. "And then I want a full explanation of what's going on here. I've held back on the questions, but the time for accounting is just around the corner."

"Meow!" Familiar said emphatically.

SYLVIE STUMBLED AWAY from the building, forgetting for a moment the need for stealth. She wanted to run. To run as fast and far as she could. Augie Marcel! What was he doing in the middle of this mess? That he was involved she didn't doubt at all.

Joey had warned her he was lurking around. But Sylvie hadn't wanted to put two and two together. How had Augie learned anything about the dolls? And how was it possible that he'd shown up in the middle of something she was involved in? In a city of twelve million people, how was it possible that he should be here, now?

She made it a block, turning into an alley, before she leaned against the wall to catch her breath and gather her wits.

Augie Marcel.

It was like a bad dream. One that had haunted her for years.

She'd left St. Mary's Orphanage with Augie Marcel when she was seventeen. Her intention was to marry him and begin to build the family she'd never had.

Even *thinking* back on those days, on her complete naïveté, was so painful she wanted to moan. She'd believed everything Augie had told her. How he was going to take care of her, how much he loved her. All of it.

But he hadn't loved her. He'd been two years older, and his quest for money had led him down a path she couldn't follow. Augie was a small-time crook. He'd run numbers and hung out with some of the bad guys, who were essentially wannabe mobsters. And it had led to trouble with the law.

As far as she knew, Augie had never been caught. At least, not while she'd been around. But she'd left, abruptly and without warning, packing her few belongings and making a run for it. She'd caught a bus to Nebraska and worked as a waitress in a café for six months, then moved on to Los Angeles, taking in whatever jobs she could find. Until she'd come back to New York to settle her score with the past.

She'd never dreamed that Augie Marcel would reappear.

Sure, he'd tried to call her a time or two, tracking her through old friends. He'd left urgent messages, but she'd never answered his calls. None of them.

Yet here he was again, right in the middle of her life. And he was hanging out with the bad guys.

What would Hunter think if he found out that she had been involved with one of the people black-mailing him?

That was the question that made her heart pound.

Hunter would never believe it was coincidence. She didn't believe it herself. But how? She'd been working at KATZ Meow. Hunter had abducted her. She'd had nothing to do with it. But he would never, never believe that.

She took some deep breaths and stepped back out onto the street and began walking. There was a bus stop not far away. She'd catch a bus and figure out how to get home. After that she didn't know what she'd do. Perhaps the best thing would be to disappear once again.

Chapter Eleven

Hunter walked Alice to her door and waited for her to unlock it. They'd spent an hour at his place waiting for Sylvie to appear. When it became apparent that she wasn't going to show up, Alice had reluctantly pointed out that she had to return home. On the way Hunter had filled her in with the details of what was happening.

Alice fumbled the keys but finally pushed the door open onto blackness. Hunter held on to the slim hope that Sylvie had gone to Alice's place. But as they both stepped into the dark apartment, he knew his hopes were in vain. Sylvie wasn't there.

He waited for Alice to check her messages and look for a note. There was no word from Sylvie.

"Now, Hunter, don't panic," Alice said, patting his arm. "Sylvie is a smart girl. Smart and quick. If they had her, they'd be in touch demanding something else. The best thing for you is to go home and wait for them to call."

Hunter knew she was right, but waiting didn't appeal to him at all. He wanted Sylvie, safe and sound. He wanted her in his arms. He'd waited in his home for what seemed like an eternity for a phone call that never came. He'd forwarded his home number to his cell phone, giving him mobility, but not what he really wanted—word from Sylvie.

"She was trying to help me," Hunter said.

"And she still is," Alice asserted. She pointed to the kitchen clock that showed after midnight. "You want some coffee?"

Hunter didn't know what he wanted. He finally shook his head. "No, I'll go home. You have to work tomorrow."

"I do," Alice said with resignation. "And Sylvie, too. She'll be there, in her little elf suit. You can be sure of that, Hunter. And when I get my hands on her, I'll make her remember how important it is to call her friends and keep them up-to-date on what's happening."

Hunter took his leave and went down to the car where Familiar waited. The black cat was the only reassuring thing in his life.

"Meow," Familiar said, patting the glove box in the car.

"No food in there," Hunter told him. He wasn't hungry, but he realized the cat hadn't eaten in several hours. Familiar was not one to miss a meal, even in a crisis.

"Meow." Familiar swatted the glove box again.

Hunter opened it to prove his point. One of Sylvie's elf gloves fell out on the floor. Familiar pounced on it, took it in his mouth and shook it.

For a long moment Hunter pondered what the cat might want. "I've called her place. She doesn't answer."

"Me-ow!" Familiar said emphatically.

"I should go there?" Hunter wasn't certain.

"Meow!" Familiar batted the key in the ignition.

"Okay. What would it hurt?" he said. "I can't do anything about the Buster Bigboy doll until they call." He felt as if everything important to him had suddenly gone wrong. He turned the car to the address that Alice had given him. It made good sense to check out her apartment. Maybe he could find some clues.

SYLVIE FOLDED one of the elf suits and put it on top of her clothes in the suitcase. It was stupid to take it along. She hated Christmas. And she hated the silly suit. But she was too tired and heartsick to try to figure out why she was taking it. She just wanted it.

Snapping the suitcase closed, she looked around the apartment. It was spartan, and even more so without the small touches of home she'd added. The place on the wall where Alice's cross-stitched sampler had hung looked so bare she had to swallow back her sudden rush of emotion. She was actually going to miss the place.

More than that, she was going to miss Hunter. She saw him clearly in her mind's eye, a man dedicated to his ideals. She'd always thought that was as big a lie as Santa Claus. He was so many things that she'd been afraid to believe in—good and honest.

She thought of the night they'd spent together and felt again the rush of desire. The mixture of passion and tenderness he'd shown was like everything she'd been afraid to dream of. She brushed a tear off her cheek. Her thirty-four years of skepticism were all for naught. In the span of a few hours, Hunter had beaten down her defenses, and the price was heartbreak.

Lugging the suitcase to the door, she determined not to indulge in such sentimental foolishness. She was doing Hunter a favor by leaving. Somehow Augie Marcel was involved in the plot against Hunter. Once Hunter learned of her connection with Augie, he'd think she'd betrayed him. It would be better for her to leave than to hang around and watch him grow to despise her.

Coward. The word echoed in her mind. That's exactly what she was. She'd rather run than stay behind and suffer the consequences. But she'd suspected all along that her past would find her. There was always a price to pay for mistakes, no matter how innocent.

Checking her watch she saw that it was just after midnight. She could call a cab and head for Grand Central. She'd take whatever train was leaving when she got there. It didn't matter where she went. One thing about starting over was that it could happen wherever she got off.

Her hand was on the knob when the doorbell rang.

Sylvie jumped back as if she'd been scalded. Her first thought was of Augie Marcel. Had he traced her to her apartment? And what did he want?

Even worse, it could be Hunter! She closed her eyes and prayed. She'd far rather face Augie.

The bell rang again, and she thought about ignoring it. When the knocking started, she forced herself to pull it open.

"I hope I'm not too late, my dear," Chester Fenton said, his blue eyes twinkling. He was nattily dressed in a wool suit and yellow-plaid vest. He held a walking cane in his hand. "I was out this way and I had a sudden inspiration. You know the Society for Prevention of Cruelty to Animals is hosting the annual Santa photo shoot tomorrow. I'm doing the honors as Santa, but I was wondering if KATZ Meow might donate your time for a day to serve as my assistant. It gets awfully cumbersome trying to manage a toddler and a cat!''

Sylvie felt as if she'd stepped into a dream. Of all the people might have expected, the old gentleman was the last. "How did you know where I lived?" She asked the first logical question that came into her head.

"You told me, my dear. Don't you recall?" His blue eyes darkened. "I've upset you, haven't I? I shouldn't barge in on people like this. I'm afraid it's something of a bad habit—just dropping in. I should have waited until morning and called, but I was so excited by the idea. You see, Santa is great in a photograph, but a truly beautiful elf, now that's something people are willing to pay good money for. And the proceeds will be split between the SPCA and the Salvation Army. Isn't that wonderful?"

"Wonderful," Sylvie agreed. She stepped back as Chester brushed past her and entered her apartment.

"Charming," he said, nodding as he looked around. "My wife was the one with the green thumb, and I can only imagine what she'd do to this place. A few yucca canes or those green lacy ferns here, some poinsettias there." He turned to her. "Have you considered a Christmas tree? After all, it is the season."

"No trees," Sylvie said, but her voice wasn't as firm as it should have been. She'd actually visualized herself trimming a tree, with Hunter handing her the ornaments.

"Are you allergic?" Chester asked.

"No," she said, amazed at the way his mind worked.

"Good!" He stepped back out the door and in a few seconds returned, a five-foot blue spruce grasped firmly in his hand. "I saw this poor little fellow outside a grocery store. It was the only one left, and I drove a hard bargain. In fact, the manager donated it to me. And since it didn't weigh much, I thought I'd bring it to you. Something told me that you were too busy to put up a tree."

"No tree," Sylvie said, her voice almost breaking. The sight of the beautiful little spruce was more than she could bear. As a child she'd wanted a tree—something exactly like the one Chester held.

"What is it, my dear?" he asked, concern furrowing his brow. "Have I upset you?"

"No tree," she said. Her gaze went to the suitcase, and his followed.

"Are you going somewhere?"

"Yes," she managed. "I'm going…"

Chester walked the tree to a corner of the room where he stood it on the makeshift stand that had been nailed to it. He came back to her and gently folded her into his arms. "What's wrong?" he asked.

Sylvie shook her head against the fabric of his vest. He smelled of cinnamon and cedar. It was an extremely comforting smell, and she inhaled slowly. "I have to go away. Something's happened."

"Is it to do with the doctor?"

Sylvie nodded. "It's a long story, but it'll be best for both of us if I leave New York."

"Are you certain of that?" Chester asked gently.

"I'm positive. You see," she looked up at him. "Hunter is the kind of man that every woman dreams about. He's good and kind and—that's not my world.''

''The past is not an address or destination,'' Chester said slowly. ''You don't have to go there unless you choose to, Sylvie.''

''I wish that were true. I keep thinking I've managed to leave it behind, and it keeps following me.''

Chester squeezed her shoulders gently. ''Come and sit down. I'll make us some hot chocolate, and you can tell me all about it.''

Sylvie started to balk, but then she realized that she wanted to talk to Chester. She wanted to tell him the truth. Somehow it didn't matter if he knew how cowardly she was. It didn't matter if she told him about wrong choices and bad decisions.

''Okay,'' she agreed, letting him lead her into the tiny kitchen.

Chester went to the refrigerator and opened the door.

''There's no milk,'' Sylvie said, remembering that she hadn't been to the store in several days.

''What's this then?'' Chester asked, pulling out a carton of milk.

Sylvie blinked. ''I thought—''

''No matter. Just have a seat. A bit of cocoa, with a dash of brandy perhaps.''

''I know I don't have any brandy, but there is some coffee liqueur.''

''Perfect,'' Chester said as he prepared the hot drinks.

As he stirred the pot of milk he turned to her. ''What are you running away from, the past or the possibility of the future?''

A quick answer rose to Sylvie's lips, but before

she could say it, she stopped herself. What was she afraid of? Not Augie or the past. She was afraid of what Hunter would think. So it was the future.

"Hunter's involved in something, because of the dolls he created. Someone's trying to steal the formula for the dolls, and they're doing it by making children sick. I hope you don't mind, but Alice filled me in on some of it earlier. She didn't have a lot of details, just enough to let me know that there's serious trouble brewing."

Sylvie wasn't surprised. "Hunter got a note demanding the formula. There's one doll that's going to cause a child to die if he doesn't give them what they want." She hesitated and then forced herself to continue. "I think I know one of the people involved." She couldn't look at Chester as she talked.

"Someone from your past?" Chester asked.

Sylvie nodded. "A man I once thought I was in love with."

"And you think Hunter will assume that you're somehow involved with this man?"

"What else could he think?" Sylvie asked. "No one in their right mind would believe it's a coincidence. I don't even believe it. Somehow, I'm involved."

"And before you'd give Hunter a chance to listen to you, you'd run away?"

Sylvie felt a flash of anger. "I don't want to hurt him. Betrayal is the cruelest of all acts. To find out that someone you trust isn't who you thought, that's worse than anything that can ever happen. I won't do that to him."

Chester poured the hot chocolate into two mugs and added a dash of the liqueur. "I'm an old man," he said slowly. "Maybe I look at things differently, but I think that you're selling Hunter short. In fact, I would say that by abandoning him now, you really are betraying him. I've seen the way he looks at you, my dear. He's invested a lot in you—his trust, his faith in you to help him." He patted her shoulder. "Think about it, Sylvie."

She wrapped her hands around the mug and felt the warmth. Instead of getting angry at Chester, she felt the tiniest hint of relief. "How is it possible that Augie Marcel is involved in trying to steal the dolls?"

"How do you know he's involved?"

"I saw him tonight. I followed the man who delivered the ransom note to Hunter. He went to this building, and while I was watching, Augie went into the building, too." Even talking about it made Sylvie's heart begin to race.

"Is it possible he went somewhere else in the building?" Chester asked reasonably.

Sylvie considered it. "It was a small building."

"And I gather that this Augie had some experience in illegal schemes." Chester made it a statement.

"In our neighborhood, survival depended on learning how to operate outside the law. Even as a young man he was connected. I finally understood that he was hooked into that way of life. Once I accepted that, I left."

Chester took a seat and scooted his chair close to her. "Drink your cocoa," he said, waiting for her to take a sip before he continued. "If this Augie is involved, you owe it to Hunter to tell him."

Sylvie sipped more chocolate. The drink was

soothing, and she felt as if she could actually think clearly. "What if, somehow, I made this happen?"

Chester's chuckle was rich and deep. "I thought you didn't believe in magic or miracles."

Sylvie frowned. "I'm not kidding."

"If I understand everything that happened, Hunter was already involved in this trouble before he came to KATZ Meow. You were drawn into this mess by accident, or happenstance. Or some people might say by fate."

At the last word Sylvie looked up. "That's it exactly! What if it's my fate to ruin his life?"

"Ah," Chester said. "Now I see exactly where the trouble is. You don't believe in any of the good miracles, only the bad."

"It's the lesson I've been taught again and again." Sylvie knew she sounded defensive, but she didn't care.

"I won't patronize you with the cup-half-full-or-half-empty analogy," Chester said. "But I insist on making it clear that life isn't a repetition of the same events. Each day, Sylvie, is a new one. You do have a choice here. You've run away once. You can do it again, but it isn't fate directing you. It's your very own choice."

The truth of his words seemed to drain her of all strength. She laced her fingers tighter around the cup and let the warmth rising from it brush her face.

"What would you do?" she finally asked.

"As I said before, I'm an old man. I'd trade the rest of my life for ten more minutes with my dear wife. So you should keep that in mind when you listen to my advice. Love is the only thing worth having, the only thing worth fighting for. If I were you I'd fight for Hunter." He took a swallow of his cocoa.

"How?"

"The only way. By telling the truth."

"You think Hunter will believe me?"

Chester considered it. "He has his own demons, and I won't pretend that he doesn't. But a relationship without trust is not worth having. Trust can be granted, initially. Then it must be earned. Hunter may doubt you, Sylvie. It's your job to make sure that he sees the truth about you."

A rush of emotion made her focus on the cocoa. "You're saying that even if I stay I might lose him. And I might hurt him."

"And he might hurt you," Chester said gently. "But if you leave, there's no other possibility. It would seem to me that the risk is well worth it."

"I don't know what I would do if he left me," Sylvie said simply. Her smile was wry. "That's it, I suppose. I'd rather leave him now than risk him turning away from me."

"Love is always a risk. Think of Hunter and his little boy." Chester gave the words a few seconds to sink in. "You can do it, Sylvie."

She blinked back her tears and swallowed the last of her chocolate. "If I stay, maybe I can help him solve this."

"I believe you can."

She looked up at the clock on the wall. It was nearly twelve-thirty. "I know he expected me to be with him. I've already let him down."

"No, you were pursuing another angle." Chester patted her hand. "You've made the right choice, my dear."

"How can you be certain?" she asked, holding is gaze.

"Now that's a trade secret." He stood up. "I must be going."

Sylvie stood up, too. She had to call Hunter and explain. It was late and she was mentally and emotionally exhausted, but she had to tell him everything before she lost her nerve. "Thank you," she said.

"You'll decorate the tree?" He looked in the corner where the little spruce stood.

"I will."

"I picked up a few things. They're outside the door." He leaned over and pecked her cheek. "You'll be fine." He retrieved his cane and coat and stepped out of the apartment into the darkened hallway.

"Shall I call a cab for you?"

"No, I enjoy the walk," he said just before he turned the corner and disappeared.

Sylvie caught the glitter of silver peeping out of a sack by the door. As she bent over to pick it up, she heard pounding footsteps on the stairs. She looked up to find Hunter racing toward her, relief so clear on his face that she merely opened her arms and let him sweep her against him.

Chapter Twelve

"You're safe," Hunter said, crushing her against him. "You're safe." She felt so delicate against his chest that he was afraid to let her go.

"I'm sorry," she murmured against his chest. "I should have called."

"Alice—we have to call Alice and let her know you're okay." He kissed the top of her head, caught again by the spicy fragrance of her hair and the sensual memories it evoked. "Where were you? What happened?"

Sylvie eased back slightly. "Come inside. There's something I have to tell you."

He knew by her tone that it wasn't good. He followed her through the door, making sure that Familiar was with them before he closed it. He was surprised to discover that now that he knew she was safe, the beginnings of anger had begun to stir. She'd worried him nearly to death.

"Let me call Alice," he said. "She was as worried as I was when we couldn't get in touch with you. Joey Monk said you were following the man who delivered the envelope."

Sylvie brought him the phone. While he was

dialing, she began to talk. "I did follow the man. He was the same one you knocked out in the toy store. Anyway, I followed him to the building, and—"

Hunter held up a finger to signal that Alice had answered. "Yes, she's fine. I'm at her place now." Hunter waited a moment. As he listened to the older woman's vocal relief, he looked at Sylvie. Her distress was so clearly written on her face. Whatever she'd been doing, it had taken a toll on her. His anger evaporated. "Thanks, Alice. I'll show her the photo right now."

He hit the off button on the phone and put it down. Reaching into his coat pocket, he took out the envelope. "I'm supposed to wait for them to call me. They sent only this." He handed it to her.

He could see that she was reluctant to even touch the envelope, but she took it, opened it and spilled the contents out into her hand.

"My God," she whispered, her face going even paler as she looked at the photograph.

"You know the child?" Hunter asked, horror and hope making him step toward her.

"Yes, I do. His name is Bobby. He comes into KATZ Meow often." Sylvie held the photo as if it might burn her. "It's Bobby."

Hunter grasped her shoulders and squeezed them. "This is wonderful," he said. "We can find the doll! We can get it before anyone is injured! What's his last name?"

Sylvie shook her head. "I don't know. He comes in with his nanny. They always pay cash." She frowned. "But I don't remember them buying a Buster Bigboy."

"Are you sure you know him?" Hunter couldn't

contain his excitement. ''Alice didn't recognize him.''

''They usually come in after four. That's when Alice normally leaves. I often stay a bit later.''

Hunter ran his hands down her shoulders. ''We can find this boy,'' he said. ''I know we can. And when we do, we can take the notes and the doll to the police and then they'll have to believe me. We have solid evidence now.''

Sylvie reached up and touched his face. Her fingertips brushed lightly over his skin, sending a chill through him. ''Maybe this will work out,'' she said, and he could tell that she, too, had caught hold of his hope.

''Tomorrow, first thing, we can find out the boy's name. We know he lives in the city. We'll be able to find him. And with a day to spare. Sylvie, this might be the best Christmas I've had in a long, long time.''

He saw the shadow of doubt in her eyes, but he knew her. She was afraid to believe that things would work out. She hadn't told him everything about her childhood, but enough for him to know that a kid whose hopes are constantly battered learns not to hope. It's the only protection such a child had from disappointment.

''Hunter, there are some things I haven't told you.''

He put his finger on her lips. ''Sylvie, I see light at the end of the tunnel. We're going to get that doll back, and then we're going to bust these guys wide open. Whoever they are, we've finally got the goods on them.'' He removed his fingers and leaned closer to her. "So I think that instead of dredging up the past, we should celebrate the future."

He could tell that his breath on her lips was having an effect. Her china-blue eyes had begun to warm, the worry replaced by desire.

"Chester said that the past was only important if I decided it was," she said.

"He's right," Hunter whispered, moving his lips a tiny bit closer. "But as much as we may need to talk about the past or think about the future, I vote for living this particular night right now, in the present."

Hunter kissed her lips, a light teasing brush. Her breathing was fast, shallow, but her shoulders beneath his hands were still tense.

He deepened the kiss, wanting the response he'd experienced the last time. Again, he felt her fighting desire.

"Is something wrong?" he asked. He drew back far enough so that he could look at her. "Do you want me to go home?"

Sylvie's blue eyes were crystal, flecked with some emotion he couldn't quite discern.

"No," she whispered. "If I told the truth, it would be that I wanted you to stay more than anything in the world."

Her words brought a thrill of pleasure to Hunter, and he swept her into his arms. This time when he kissed her, he held nothing back. And he felt her yield, opening herself to him with complete abandon.

Hunter knew the emotions he was feeling were very dangerous. Every minute he spent with Sylvie strengthened his deep feelings for her. He was falling hard and fast, and he didn't care.

His fingers moved to the buttons of her blouse and in a moment it fell to the floor. She slid his jacket from his shoulders, then turned her attention to his shirt. In record time they stood in a pool of clothing, until Sylvie took his hand and led him to the bedroom.

AHH, SWEET MYSTERY OF LIFE, etcetera, etcetera. I'm glad to see that the two humanoids are strengthening the bond of love. But I wish the phone would ring. This cat is ready for some action.

I don't know if Hunter has recognized the packed suitcase at the door. If I were a muscle cat, I might try moving it to a closet. It's only going to make trouble in the future, if I know anything about human nature.

Let me take a sniff around. Chester Fenton has been here. Now that's one unusual humanoid. There's something very different about that old man. Good different, not bad. He was in the kitchen for a while. Cinnamon, cedar, chocolate and…coffee liqueur. A nice combination of the good things in life.

I'll saunter back in here and look at that photo again. Let's see, a little paw work and I have it. Cute kid. But there's more to the photo than that. It was taken in Central Park. I recognize the locale. That's easy to spot, though I doubt my little sprite and the good doctor have made that observation.

So whoever snapped the picture happened to catch the little boy out and about, or else they were keeping him. So it could be the caregiver, or a stranger who's been stalking the boy.

Sylvie has seen the child in the store with a caregiver who pays cash. This is all pertinent, but I'm

*not so certain even I can figure out what it means.
And from what I can tell about my sprite and the
good doctor, they're caught up in another mystery.
One that has totally absorbed them.*

*You know, I love to see love at work, but there are
times when it makes me want to be at home with
Clotilde. It's almost Christmas, and I found the perfect gift for her. What frisky femme fatale wouldn't
love a battery-operated, catnip-stuffed mouse? The
little dickens has a computer chip embedded in it so
that he rushes around the room exactly like a real
mouse.*

*Heh, heh, and when she gets tired of chasing it,
she can turn it loose during one of her humanoid's
fancy dinner parties. Talk about a good time!
Me-ow! Even more fun than chasing a mouse is
watching women in four-inch heels squeal and jump
up on chairs. Yes, I can see that New Year's Eve has
plenty of potential.*

*But first I have to conclude the Serial Santa case.
The holidays won't be enjoyable at all if some innocent child is injured. But that won't happen. Not
with Familiar on the case.*

SYLVIE SLIPPED FROM the bed, hoping not to disturb
Hunter. She'd fallen asleep for half an hour, but
she'd awakened in the midst of a bad dream.

She went to the window and pushed back the
gauzy curtain. The scene outside her small window
wasn't much different from what Hunter awakened
to each morning. The difference was that he'd chosen
to live on Thirty-fourth Street. She had rented what
she could afford. She turned to look at him. Window
light filtered over the bed and gave him the look of

a statue carved in cool stone. The sight of him, muscled and lean with dark hair curling on his chest, made her want him with an intensity that was almost painful.

He was so handsome and so unaware of it. He was one of those rare people who focused outside himself almost all the time. Was that because he'd grown up in a world that encouraged such a way of thinking?

Once again she found herself thinking of the differences that separated them. Only when she was in his arms did it seem they could bridge that gulf. But she was smart enough to know that passion and desire weren't the mortar to solidify a good relationship.

She closed her eyes, remembering the dream. In it she'd been seventeen, a girl with big blue eyes and black hair that hung to her waist. She was in St. Mary's and wanted nothing more than to be out. In the dream she'd been standing in a window, looking outside. And Augie Marcel had been walking up to the orphanage. He'd come looking for her.

Only this time she knew that she was making a mistake. Yet she still put her clothes in her single suitcase and went out to meet him. Even knowing that it was wrong, she had done it anyway.

That's what had awakened her. Knowing that she was capable of willfully doing the wrong thing.

She knew her conscience was bothering her. She had to tell Hunter about Augie. Even though it looked as if they might be able to figure things out without such a revelation, she had to tell him. For her own sake. And she would, as soon as he woke up.

"Sylvie?"

Hunter's voice called to her sleepily. It was one of the most wonderful sounds she'd ever heard.

"What's wrong? Can't you sleep?"

"I'm okay," she said, going back to the bed and leaning forward to kiss him. She would tell him now. With the pale light washing over them, she would tell him and it would be okay.

"I saw the tree. Why don't we decorate it?" Hunter asked, pushing himself to a sitting position.

"Now?"

"Why not? You can't sleep and tomorrow, or today I should say, is Christmas Eve. We might not get another chance."

Sylvie glanced at the bedside clock. It was 3:00 a.m. There was so little time left. The vision she'd had of them decorating the tree together came back to her. It was a fantasy, and one that might never present itself again. "Let's do it," she said.

"When did you have time to buy a tree?" Hunter asked, reaching out and stroking her back.

"Chester brought it to me." She smiled at the memory. "I've never had a tree before."

"Then let's make this one count." He kicked away the few covers that had been on his legs. "You know Santa would be unhappy if he came to see you and there weren't any decorations."

Sylvie put her hand on his chest, feeling the beating of his heart. "Do you have a tree?"

He chuckled. "No, not since Brad died. But maybe I can share yours. What do you think?"

"I think that's a definite yes. Would you like some breakfast?"

"You can't expect a man to decorate unless you feed him."

"Then I'll get busy in the kitchen." Even as she said it, Sylvie felt a chuckle coming on. "I never thought I'd say those words."

"Life has a strange way of making us change," he said. "And sometimes, it's all for the best."

She slipped into her favorite terry cloth robe while Hunter grabbed his slacks and an old sweatshirt she found for him. She went to the kitchen to make coffee and raid the refrigerator while he examined the tree, finding the best side.

After a breakfast of scrambled eggs and toast, they went into the small living room. Sylvie looked at the bag of decorations with a wary eye.

"The lights go on first," Hunter prompted.

Sylvie found the colored twinkle lights at the bottom of the bag and together they wound them through the spicy branches of the spruce.

"Look," she said, reaching into a tangle of garland and pulling out a tape. "It's Christmas music."

"Now that would be festive," Hunter said, dangling a strand of garland in front of Familiar. The black cat batted the garland, then grabbed it and took off.

Sylvie watched the cat's antics with one eyebrow cocked. "He's playing you for a fool," she warned Hunter. "Give him half a chance and he'll have you chasing around like a trained seal."

"Not on your life."

But the words were hardly out of his mouth before Familiar upended a box of glass ornaments and sent them rolling across the carpet and under chairs and the sofa.

"Right," Sylvie said, laughing out loud as Hunter scrambled after them. "We've quickly established who's master of this house.'' This was better than she'd ever imagined.

She popped the tape into her player and grinned big at the first bars of ''Frosty the Snowman.'' The song prompted her to look out the window.

''Hunter!'' She pointed. The first big flakes of snow had just begun to fall.

''It looks like a white Christmas for sure,'' Hunter said. ''I couldn't have ordered it better.''

While tiny drifts of snow collected against the windowpanes, together they collected the ornaments and hung them on the tree. Chester's sack was packed amazingly full. Whenever Hunter suggested something, Sylvie examined the contents of the bag and found it. After the ornaments they strung the silver tinsel garlands that gave the little tree the final touch of holiday glitter.

''Perfect,'' Sylvie said, feeling like a princess as Hunter slipped his arm around her shoulders. They both stood back to admire the tree.

''Perfect,'' Hunter agreed. ''Just like you,'' he said, leaning over to kiss her ear. ''I know what I want for Christmas.''

''Would you settle for an early present?'' she asked.

''Only if you'll wear your elf suit.''

''That could be arranged, but only for you.'' She lifted her face for his kiss.

EGADS, THEY'RE AT IT AGAIN. Now, I'm all for the expression of love, but we have work to do. They had their fun with the tree, and now it's time for work. We need to get busy.

I suppose the thing to do is somehow get their

attention. A gentle nip on the shin always works. I'll pick the sprite. Her legs are bare and she is a bit tastier.

One easy little nip and her mind is off Hunter and right where it belongs. On me. So a dash for the photo. Now I have both of their attention.

Even though I'm putting my paw on the pertinent details in the photo, they don't seem to be able to get it. Let's see, how can I communicate with them. Brak would know exactly what I wanted, but he's in Texas and there's no time to make a call.

I've given this some thought, and finding Bobby isn't going to be as easy as the humanoids think. The criminal element wouldn't have chosen a child so easily traced, unless they were certain that the path was blocked. So we have to get to work now.

I see a light dawning in Hunter's eyes. He's got it, by George! He's putting two and two together and coming up with four. Now he's got Sylvie excited. This is going to be okay. They're talking good sense now. Sylvie is trying to remember more about the nanny.

She's the key, I do believe.

All we have to do is find her, and if she doesn't know where Bobby and the doll are, I'll make her talk. Few women can endure the old sandpaper tongue on the backs of their knees. She'll be singing like the proverbial stool pigeon once I get hold of her.

Then I can resolve this case and get back to D.C., where Clotilde has hung mistletoe over the little kitty door.

Chapter Thirteen

Hunter wasn't certain that going after hours to KATZ Meow twice in a row was a good idea. Dawn was breaking, and the city was the quietest he'd ever seen it. The newly fallen snow was like a blessing, covering everything ugly and unpleasant—a façade for what lay beneath the pristine white blanket. He drove slowly along the streets, listening to Sylvie's plan and trying hard to ignore the foreboding that gathered in his gut.

"There are videotapes of all purchases," Sylvie said, so excited that her words seemed to spill out. "They keep the tapes for about a month. That woman and the little boy were in the store not a week ago. I can find the video and we'll have a picture of the woman. We can go to the police with that. It's enough with the photograph of the child and the blackmail note. I'm certain they'll listen to us!"

Hunter wasn't so certain. They had evidence, but it was all things anyone could produce. Not a single piece of evidence they had was conclusive. He'd learned, very quickly, that police work started with a crime. Just like medicine started with a disease. Most doctors—and policemen—wanted to work from the end backward. Prevention was a word politicians bandied about during campaigns for reelection and pseudo nutritionists made rash promises about with miracle foods.

"Hunter?"

He glanced over at Sylvie. "Sorry," he said. "I was thinking."

"We're here." She pointed to the store. "We should park."

"I don't know." Hunter pulled across the street and looked at the store. In the past hour, the snow had fallen thick and fast. With all of the Christmas lights in the window and the giant neon tabby cat that danced, it did look like a place where Santa might shop for toys. As magical as the store looked, he still had a sense of impending doom. "We were lucky the first time. I'm sure they've increased security."

"I'm an employee. I have a key. Maybe I'm a little overeager on Christmas Eve, but I want to make sure the shelves are ready for that last-minute rush."

Looking at her in the pale blue light that reflected off the new snow, Hunter loved her more intensely than he ever thought possible.

"You're sure you want me to wait in the car?" This was the part he disliked the most.

"Positive." He caught the hint of stubbornness in her beautiful eyes. He was in for a lifetime of negotiation—Sylvie was about as mulish as a woman could get. And he loved even that.

"You've got an hour," he said. "No more. If you aren't back in this car in an hour, I'm coming in for you."

"Don't park. Drive around so it's not obvious you're waiting," Sylvie said.

"Okay." He liked this even less, but it made sense.

"I work in this store every day. I'll lock the door behind me this time. It's perfectly safe." She leaned across the seat, kissed his cheek and darted out of the car before he could change his mind.

The snow was still falling, and Hunter watched as she dashed across the empty street and headed toward the employee entrance. She was so much a child, in her movements and her energy. Even though she'd been badly hurt, she'd maintained that quicksilver element that would keep her always youthful.

In the blink of an eye she'd disappeared, leaving only the strange little footprints from her elf boots.

Hunter couldn't help but compare her to his former wife. Connie had been blond and cool and professional. She'd been the woman he'd never expected to catch. Even after they were married and Brad was born, Hunter always had the feeling that one day he would come home and Connie would be gone. Her closets of expensive clothes empty, her shoe racks stripped bare.

He wasn't surprised when it happened.

For even though she'd married him and borne his son, he'd never really had her. Connie was unattainable. Or she had been for him. He could only hope that the future gave her what she wanted.

Sylvie had taught him how good loving another person could be, and he wanted that for everyone. To go through life without that feeling now seemed unendurable.

Staring at the storefront display, he watched a two-foot ballerina-cat dance on a pedestal. It was a plump gray tabby, so hefty it didn't have a neck. It danced with great vigor, but not much grace—all in all, very amusing. He grinned at the idea of Familiar's reaction. The cat wouldn't like it. Not one little bit. Familiar wasn't one to tolerate a mocking type of humor where felines were concerned.

The nagging sense of disaster returned. It was odd, but the cat had insisted on staying at Sylvie's house. Neither Hunter nor Sylvie had been able to coax him along.

As peculiar as Familiar had been, there was something else troubling him. The suitcase beside the door. He hadn't asked any questions, but it looked as if Sylvie was planning on leaving town. It was a pretty big suitcase. And he'd seen where several things had been taken off the wall leaving empty nails.

It was impossible that she'd been about to leave. She wasn't like that. She wasn't the kind who would disappear. Not in the middle of this blackmail scheme when children were at risk.

She wasn't anything like his ex-wife.

He hadn't known her long, but he knew her well enough to know she wouldn't cut and run. That wasn't Sylvie West.

Yet he hadn't asked her. And she'd offered no explanation.

Maybe the luggage had been filled with Christmas gifts. Her apartment was small, and perhaps it was a way of storage. He tried to think of logical reasons. But his mind held on to the image of the case sitting at the door, as if she intended to pick it up at any moment and walk out.

Hunter checked the time. He'd been sitting for five minutes, and he could see a security guard staring out the front window at him. He started the car and made a left at the next corner. He intended to drive aimlessly, to kill the time until Sylvie was ready for him to get her. But the car headed straight back to her apartment.

As he climbed the stairs he knew what he was doing was wrong, yet he couldn't stop himself. All he had to do was ask her, he argued with himself. One simple question was all it would take.

He wasn't willing to risk that question, though. Sylvie was extremely touchy in some areas. To imply that he thought she was a coward would do irrevocable damage. The smartest thing was to look—and put his anxieties to rest.

When he unlocked the door of the apartment, there was a strange scuttling. Instantly alert, Hunter opened the door on chaos. The suitcase was wide open in front of him and Sylvie's things were strewn about the floor.

His first reaction was that someone had broken into the apartment and searched it for something.

And then he saw Familiar, a red blouse in his mouth, sneaking toward the bedroom.

UH-OH. CAUGHT IN THE ACT. I'd hoped to be able to get most of her stuff back in the bedroom before they returned. I never dreamed Hunter would come back here. But judging from the look on his face, he was worried about that suitcase.

Now all of his fears have been confirmed.

Drat! I didn't have enough time. So now what I need is a new game plan. I wonder how to conjure up a sick aunt in Toledo for Sylvie. She's going to need a good reason for this, and she's going to need it fast.

I could only wish the blackmailers would call with their instructions. That would keep Hunter occupied until I figure out a way to smooth over this little love mess. No such luck!

As much as I enjoy playing cupid, I am far more experienced as the feline Sherlock. As a trained observer of human contretemps, I know that mayhem, mystery and the strange muddling of the heart are often companions. Enough musing—time for action.

AS SHE'D THOUGHT, Sylvie had no difficulty getting into KATZ Meow, or in finding the video records. But the massive quantity of tape was disheartening. Though she had narrowed the time down to several days and the tapes were clearly marked for different areas of the store, it was still an impressive amount of tape she needed to view.

Time was the enemy.

She made sure the security guards—an increased force since the last incident in the store—were elsewhere, and then she set up the computer and began to fast-forward through the tapes that involved her sales area.

After a night with virtually no sleep, Sylvie found the images of people rushing around the store to be mesmerizing, then lulling. She stood up to keep from falling asleep. She didn't have time to watch the tapes on normal speed, and she had to be alert to catch the image of the nanny and young boy with the images rushing across the screen.

She finished the third tape and checked her watch.

She had forty minutes left. The impossibility of what she was trying to do almost overwhelmed her. Instead of giving up, she tightened her jaw and put another tape in.

Glaring at the screen, she focused.

At first she didn't believe what she saw. She slowed the fast motion, rewound slightly and watched again. The woman she recognized as the nanny came up to the register but the image wasn't clear! The woman was tall, curvaceous and poised, but no matter how she focused, Sylvie couldn't make out her features.

She played the tape forward and watched as the woman and the boy moved away. Before they were out of range, Clarise Blalock appeared. The young boy turned, then rushed to Clarise. She swept him into her arms and kissed him.

Sylvie wasn't an expert at body language, but she knew instantly that the toddler was more than a favorite customer to Mrs. Blalock. The boy was her son.

The child in danger was Bobby Blalock, son of the owner of KATZ Meow. She recognized the mother's features in the boy's face.

The perfection of the plan was instantly clear to Sylvie. If Hunter didn't give them what they wanted, they'd picked the perfect child to use as a weapon, and the perfect season.

It was all so very clever.

And it smacked of Augie Marcel.

HUNTER STEPPED OVER the contents of the suitcase and went to the nearest chair and sat down. He should have expected this. He had expected it. But he hadn't believed it.

He looked at the clothes and shoes scattered where the cat had dragged them. Most damning of all were the photographs and the wall decorations. Sylvie was leaving, and it wasn't for a vacation. She'd planned on never coming back.

Why?

That was the question that haunted him as he felt Familiar's paws on his leg.

"Meow." Familiar rubbed against him, offering comfort.

"You were trying to hide the evidence, weren't you?" Hunter asked, not even able to focus on the cat's unusual behavior. "She was leaving when I came in here last night. And she never said a word."

Images from the night came back to him. Sylvie had been incredible. Her passion was real—he would be willing to risk his life on that. She wasn't faking her feelings for him. So why had she packed her things, ready for flight?

"Me-ow." Familiar lightly extended his claws into Hunter's leg.

Hunter didn't even react. He was numb, for all practical purposes. It wasn't until the cat swatted him, hard, that Hunter remembered to look at his watch. Whatever else he had to do, he had to get back to the store to pick up Sylvie.

Familiar ran to the door and clawed at it.

"You're right," he said, rising abruptly. "She didn't leave. That's the most important thing. And she's put herself in danger to help me."

Familiar arched his back, tail flicking, and gave a low growl that ended in a sharp meow.

Hunter didn't waste any more time. He and the cat dashed from the apartment to the car. It was still early enough that traffic was light, and he drove with speed and determination.

"She didn't leave," he said. "But I wonder what stopped her."

"Meow, meow, meow…meow, meow, meow."

Hunter risked a look at the cat. "Jingle Bells?"

The cat gave him a glare.

"Christmas?"

Familiar blinked twice quickly.

"It doesn't make sense to me, but if that's what you say. Right now I think we have to focus on finding Bobby Whoever-he-is. After that, I'm going to have a long talk with Sylvie. Whatever it is that frightens her, we're going to work it out."

It wasn't yet seven o'clock, but already the stores were beginning to show signs of life as employees came in early to prepare for the Christmas rush. Hunter pressed harder on the gas. The dark feeling of foreboding intensified. He drove faster.

The cat sat perched on the edge of the seat staring out the front window with an intensity that only made Hunter more anxious.

He pulled up in front of KATZ Meow, lucky to find a parking place even at seven o'clock. In the storefront window, the tabby ballerina cat danced away. The neon gleamed brilliantly against the pinkening sky and the white snow. It was a scene as peaceful and pretty as a postcard.

Hunter knew he should feel better, but he didn't.

He checked his watch. He was five minutes early. So he decided he would wait. Even though every second would be an eternity.

"Meow!" Familiar scratched at the window.

"Not yet," he said.

"Meow!" Familiar popped the glass hard.

Hunter shook his head. "Four more minutes."

Familiar hurled himself at the glass, then did it again.

Hunter opened the door and let the cat out. Familiar bounded across the snowy street and headed straight for the toy store. Hunter was only a few yards behind him, dread growing with every step.

At the employee's entrance, Hunter tried to push through the door. It opened, but he'd gone no farther than five steps when a uniformed guard stepped directly into his path.

"I'm looking for Sylvie West," Hunter explained before the man could ask a question.

"What department?"

Hunter didn't have the right answer. "Toddlers, but—"

"Employees don't come in until nine," the man said.

"She's here. I brought her here early, to get ready to open. Could I just look to make sure she's okay?"

"Why wouldn't she be?" The guard was looking at him with wary concern. "You're not here to make trouble with your girlfriend, are you?" His gaze shifted over Hunter's body, searching for the knife or gun that would indicate domestic violence was what was on Hunter's mind.

"She's my friend. I'm concerned for her. That's all."

"Wait outside. I'll look."

Hunter stepped outside. His only hope was that Familiar had made it past the guard. The last Hunter had seen of the cat, he was rushing down the corridor. If anyone could find Sylvie, it was Familiar.

As Hunter paced, he stepped into the new snow. It was light and crisp and perfect for the holiday. He tried to focus on the snow as he waited for the guard or Familiar, or better than those options, Sylvie, to appear.

He was growing impatient when the security guard finally returned. "We searched the store, top to bottom. There's no one here named Sylvie West."

"Maybe she didn't hear you. Maybe she was in the bathroom." Hunter watched the guard closely.

"She isn't here."

"How can you be so certain? You don't even know what she looks like."

The guard reached into the pocket of his uniform and drew out a piece of paper. "She has black hair, blue eyes and is a very pretty woman. She isn't here."

"Just let me look around."

The guard's eyes narrowed. "Look, buddy, we looked through the whole store. She isn't here. Now there's nothing else I can tell you. Get lost, before I have to call the cops and get them to move you along."

"Please listen to me." Hunter reached into his pocket for the photo of the child. "There's a young boy in danger…"

The security guard stepped inside. Though the thick glass, Hunter could still hear him. "Tell it to the cops," he said wearily. "We have enough going on right now. We don't need some nutcase creating work for us."

He turned abruptly and walked away. Hunter tried

the door again, but it was locked. Familiar was locked in, and he was locked out.

But where was Sylvie?

He had to find out if she'd decided to cut and run.

Chapter Fourteen

Sylvie walked up to the gate of the Candlewick complex with a swagger. "Mrs. Blalock is expecting me," she told the guard, who lifted both eyebrows in amusement.

"You're the first of her guests ever to arrive on foot," he said with a grin. "To my knowledge, no one has ever arrived wearing green boots that turn up at the toes." His gaze roved up her legs.

Sylvie rued the decision to wear her elf suit. It had been a poor choice all around, even though it had made sense when she'd thought she might actually go to work. But then she hadn't been thinking clearly at all.

"I'm doing some favors for Mrs. Blalock," Sylvie said with as much dignity as she could muster. "Tell her it's about Bobby."

The guard went to the intercom and spoke softly into it. Though Sylvie craned her neck and did her best to listen, she couldn't overhear the conversation. When he came back to her, she was surprised to see that lines marked his forehead.

"Come inside here and warm up before you freeze," he said, opening the door of the guardhouse.

"I have some fresh coffee and my wife sent some homemade cranberry cake."

Sylvie was sorely tempted. She was freezing and hungry. Her three o'clock breakfast was long gone, and the elf suit, though cute, wasn't very warm.

Still, she didn't like the idea of entering the security building. The guard was being just a little *too* nice. She'd accepted that Hunter might actually be a nice man, but she wasn't buying into the idea that every Tom, Dick or Harry on the street wanted to warm her up with coffee and feed her holiday cake out of the goodness of his heart. "I'm okay. Is Mrs. Blalock coming to get me?" Her only hope was that the woman would be intrigued enough to come and investigate.

"There's a problem. Mrs. Blalock is out of town. The maid said she'd been gone for two days and hasn't called in to check for her messages." The guard's frown deepened. "That really isn't like her. She calls me every day when she's away. I assumed that she was going in to work early and staying late." He turned a speculative gaze on Sylvie. "Is there something you aren't telling me?"

Sylvie felt a rush of adrenaline. "The little boy, Bobby. Have you seen him?"

Instantly the guard was alert. "I haven't seen Bobby for the past day or two." He looked at her. "What's going on here?"

Sylvie debated telling the truth, but Hunter's experience warned her that people weren't likely to believe her. "I'm supposed to pretend to be an elf. You know, for a party. A holiday surprise party for her little boy. I'm sure Mrs. Blalock said today, but I guess I could be wrong."

The guard eyed her with renewed suspicion. Her mention of the child had triggered his warning system. "Let me make some calls," he said slowly.

Sylvie, too, went on alert. "Maybe I should go check my calendar. I must have gotten the date wrong." She had to get out of there, and fast. One of the calls the guard intended to make would be to the police. She was certain of that.

"Not so fast." The guard reached out and caught her sleeve. "I think you should stay right here until we figure out what's going on. Something isn't right here, and if you're a part of it, then you're going to have some explaining to do."

He lifted the telephone receiver to his mouth. "Yes, this is Charlie down at the main gate of Candlewick. We've got ourselves a little problem."

He looked down at his desk for a split second, and Sylvie took off running. She nearly tripped over a snowbank before she darted into the thick trees at the side of the road.

She heard the door of the guardhouse open and the sound of his leather boots on the pavement.

"Halt!" he called out. "Hey, you'd better stop!"

But Sylvie kept running deeper and deeper into the surrounding thicket of trees. In the silence of the snow-covered woods, she ran as hard as she could, knowing that she left a clear path behind for anyone who chose to come after her.

Her hope was that the guard wouldn't leave his post. He might think she was a decoy sent to lure him away. Her plan was to run into the woods and then veer back to the right, coming out on the road half a mile or so west of Candlewick. But the woods were thick, and her elf boots were a hindrance in the crusty snow. Time and time again she had to stop and retrieve one. Though she was tempted to leave them behind, she knew that to try to make it barefoot would be insane.

She struggled on, listening intently for the sound of sirens, trying to decide whether it would be best to wait it out in the woods. The cops could track her, but maybe they would think she wasn't worth the trouble. How dangerous could an elf be? But she knew she was only playing games with herself to try to assuage the fear that was steadily growing.

She also didn't have time to waste. She had to get to Hunter. She'd discovered the identity of the little boy—and that was the most important thing. If Hunter could retrieve Buster Bigboy, then the forces against him would have no hold on him.

Once that was resolved, she and Hunter could make the time to discuss her past, and his. One thing her near flight the night before had taught her was that she had to confront the past. If Hunter was there to help her, she thought she might have the courage to do it.

Through the thinning trees, she caught a flash of red as a big car sped down the road. She'd never been a girl scout, but her sense of direction was good. She'd accurately chosen the path, and she felt a sense of relief and accomplishment.

She edged closer to the road while still keeping to thick cover. She had to make sure that when she stepped out to flag a ride, it wouldn't be with the cops.

Her vantage point was good. She was tucked behind a large sycamore trunk and could see the roadway clearly. In the distance a black sports car was headed her way. It was a fancy car. One of the very expensive ones. It fit perfectly in the neighborhood.

She was gathering herself to make a dash out to the road when her boot snagged on a root buried beneath the snow. She bent down to try and pull it free, looking up to see that the car was rapidly approaching. She tugged, losing her patience, but the boot held firm.

Giving one mighty heave, she found herself tumbling backward in the snow. She was free, though. She jumped up and started toward the road when the car rounded a curve and a shaft of sunlight illuminated the driver.

She froze in midleap, dropping down to her hands and knees.

The man driving the car was Augie Marcel.

I HAVE BEEN IN EVERY ROOM, every nook and cranny of KATZ Meow. The security guard wasn't lying. Sylvie isn't here. But she's been here. And she hasn't been gone long. There's still a lingering trace of that delicious bath soap she uses. Gardenia? Enough about soap. The million-dollar question is, where has Sylvie gone?

I thought for sure Chester had worked his magic on her last night. Of course I wasn't privy to that conversation, but as a cat with deductive abilities, I could easily recreate the entire scenario. Imagination and a sharp eye are the two best tools a detective has.

I can picture the way Chester slipped the tree in on her—the soothing hot chocolate. I noticed the way the chairs were drawn up at the table so they could talk. Old Chester may be a little strange, but he has a way with people. And he has a good heart. If it hadn't been for him, I fear Sylvie would have been long gone.

But why was she running away? And where has she gone to now? I'm going to have to change her nickname from the sprite to the gingerbread girl.

I don't like this continual disappearing act. Not one little bit.

Heavy footsteps in the corridor. The security guy has passed by, so maybe I'll gather a few facts in here. The video machine is still on. The tape is slotted in it. Geez, she left in a hurry. She didn't even bother to cover her tracks. So let's punch play.

Eureka! There's the curly haired little boy, hanging on to the arm of the woman who must be the nanny. I think I should rewind a tad. I'd like to know the last thing Sylvie saw before she tore out of this store without waiting for the good doctor or me.

Now I have the boy. And he's rushing to that well-dressed woman. She's the child's mother, plain as day. And she's obviously someone who's in charge in the store.

This is beginning to make more and more sense. And I'm liking it less and less.

I wish this machine had some device to print out the picture, but I don't see it. Technology is a necessary evil as far as I'm concerned. I've learned the basics, but new developments occur so fast that not even a cat as smart as I am can keep up.

I'll just have to rely on the old-fashioned method. Memory and the hope that Hunter isn't so overwrought he won't listen to me.

We have to find out who this woman is. And we have to find her son.

Wait a minute, Billybob. I have an idea. If she works in the store, she's bound to be in the employee files. Since I'm already knee-deep in breaking and entering, I can stay a little longer. Hunter will wait for me.

Since there's no evidence that Sylvie looked anything else up, I'd say that she knew the woman. From the style of dress and the five-hundred-dollar shoes she's wearing, I'd say she's definitely in upper management. That's where I'll start.

Here're the files. And there she is, right at the top of the front page. Clarise Blalock, owner of KATZ Meow! Me-ow! That's the right word.

The pieces of the puzzle are coming together. The picture is clear but awfully ugly. Now I'll snatch this bio of Mrs. Blalock and I'll be on my way.

Just in time, too. Here comes security!

HUNTER HAD STOMPED a mud puddle in the snow as he paced and waited for Familiar to return. He felt the need for action, but he had nowhere to go. And he didn't want to abandon the cat. Besides, if any leads were going to turn up, he was convinced they would come from Familiar.

It was nearly seven-thirty, and Hunter was growing more and more concerned that he hadn't received a phone call with the latest instructions. The clock was ticking. In less than twenty-four hours, little Bobby would undoubtedly be opening his Christmas presents. If the Buster Bigboy was truly contaminated with a toxic substance, the child could be dead in less than a day.

The more Hunter thought about it, the faster he paced. He understood the psychology of the long silence. The men who wanted his formula wanted to leave him twisting in the wind—to imagine the sickness and death of the child in the photograph in order to soften him up for the blackmail. It was the cruelest form of torture.

By the time they did call him, they expected that his own imagination would have done most of the work. He would be ripe for the picking. Or at least that's what they would hope.

Even though he knew the strategy behind the silence, it troubled him that they hadn't called. What if something had gone wrong? What if the child had gotten into the toy before Christmas? What if the ingredients they used weren't stable and the doll had poisoned the entire family? With a toxic substance, nothing could be taken for granted.

And where was Sylvie? Had something dreadful happened to her?

His mind was spinning when Familiar dashed toward him, a piece of white paper in the cat's mouth.

"What's that?" Hunter asked, bending down to the cat. But Familiar darted across the street toward the car. Hunter followed, taking note that traffic had increased considerably. It was, after all, the day before Christmas.

Familiar was in the car before Hunter could snatch the paper. He looked at it. It was a copy of a photograph and bio. The woman was dark-haired, pretty, and very elegant. Sadness haunted her eyes.

Familiar found the photograph of the boy and gave it to Hunter with a muffled meow.

It took a few seconds, but Hunter finally understood. "This is the boy's mother. Clarise Blalock. Owner of KATZ Meow," Hunter said, reading the bio sheet the cat had provided. He knew instantly that Sylvie had gone after the woman. She must have come out while he'd been at her apartment. He could kick himself.

He stepped on the gas. "I know where Candlewick is," Hunter said. "Connie always wanted to live in that neighborhood. She said it was the place for up-and-coming professionals."

As he pulled out into the flow of traffic, he almost slammed on the brakes. He hadn't thought about it, but the woman he'd followed from Joey Monk's bar, The Jungle Room, had gone to the entrance of Candlewick. He'd followed her there.

As he shifted from lane to lane of the intensifying traffic, Hunter tried to examine the photograph of the woman pictured on the page Familiar had brought him.

She didn't look like the redhead in the bar, but he couldn't say for absolute certain. Dark glasses, a wig, it was impossible to say in the dim lighting of the bar.

If Clarise Blalock were somehow involved in the blackmail scheme, then the boy really wasn't in any danger.

That thought was so wonderful that Hunter gripped the steering wheel and focused his attention on driving even faster. As awful as it was for a mother to use the threat of injury to her child as a tool of blackmail, Hunter just wanted the boy to be safe.

But he couldn't be certain. He couldn't risk that Clarise Blalock wasn't an involuntary player. It was as likely that she, too, was being blackmailed into participating in the scheme. What mother wouldn't do anything to save her child? If that was the case, he would certainly understand.

Even though the snow was treacherous, Hunter drove fast. Manhattan was generally tall buildings, masses of people and traffic, but there were sections where the woods were thick and the sense of isolation was carefully maintained.

Candlewick was one of these exclusive neighborhoods. He drove to the brick building at the entrance to the exclusive community. Security guards remained on duty day and night.

"Mrs. Blalock, please," Hunter said to the guard who approached the car. "I'm Dr. Hunter Semmes, here to see her son, Bobby."

He didn't like the look in the guard's eyes. "She called you?" he asked.

"I have information for her regarding Bobby." Hunter wanted to be careful. Obviously the guard was on to something.

"Maybe you'd like to share that information with the police," the guard said. "Just pull right over here. They're on their way."

"What's wrong?" Hunter asked.

"There's an awful lot of interest in Bobby Blalock, and the mother and child are missing. I hope to God they're not hurt, because if they are…" The guard didn't finish the threat.

Hunter met the man's gaze. "I'm afraid they're in danger." He gathered up the Polaroid picture of the boy and the bio of the mother that Familiar had taken from the store. "I'm being blackmailed, and this is the child that I've been told will be injured if I don't cooperate. Is this Bobby Blalock?" he asked.

"That's him," the guard acknowledged. "You're

being blackmailed? What's you're connection to the Blalocks?''

''None that I know of.'' He pulled a card from his pocket and handed it to the guard with all of the gathered information, including the blackmail note. ''I am Hunter Semmes. I've been to the police with a report of my problem, but they thought I was just another nut.''

The guard took the bundle.

Hunter continued. ''Someone has poisoned dolls that I've made.'' He held up a warning hand to halt the man from interrupting. ''Believe me or not, I don't care what you think. I'm telling the truth. And I'm looking for a woman, dark hair, blue eyes.'' He saw by the guard's expression that Sylvie had been there.

''Elf suit?''

''That's her. Where is she?''

''She took off into the woods,'' he said, shrugging. ''That's why I called the police.''

Hunter looked into the snow-covered woods. He had to get to Sylvie. She might freeze to death, and this buffoon was just pointing to the woods as if she weren't in danger. ''Just give all the information to the police,'' Hunter said as he threw the car into Reverse.

''You can tell them yourself—''

''I think not.'' Hunter spun out. He didn't have time to waste with the authorities. He'd already learned that filling out reports and talking to different officers took time he didn't have.

He sped down the road. Just as he was making a curve, a flash of green darted out of the woods. It wasn't a deer—and it didn't look like any other animal. He braked suddenly, almost skidding.

Then he recognized her. Sylvie! She was running toward the car. He opened the passenger door and she threw herself into the vehicle.

Hunter wanted to kiss her. Her pale skin was almost blue with cold, and he saw that her green boots were a sodden mess. Her feet would be completely frozen. "Sylvie, are you okay?" He slowed long enough to reach across the seat and touch her. She was shaking.

"Just go," she said. "Go fast."

"What is it?" Hunter asked as he complied with her demand.

"We have to find out where Mrs. Blalock is," Sylvie said, righting herself in the seat and hugging Familiar as he snuggled on her lap.

"She isn't home," Hunter said, "but I suspect you already know that."

"Did the guard give you a clue where she might be?"

"No." Hunter saw the blue lights flashing in the distance, heading toward him. The police. He wondered if the security guard had given them a description of his car. If so, then he was going to give them a run for their money.

"Hold on," he told Sylvie.

She watched the police cars approaching. There were three of them, siren blazing. "Don't try to outrun them," she said.

"If we're taken into custody, that boy may die."

She put a hand on his arm, and Hunter felt the tremble in her fingers. "Maybe they'll help us."

"I left word with the guard. He can tell them everything they need to know. But I can't take a risk that they'll believe me this time. They haven't before.'' Hunter glanced at her. Her face was grim as she braced in the seat. But she was willing to trust his judgment, and that made his heart beat even faster.

The lead patrol car had begun to slow.

''They're going to try to stop you,'' Sylvie said. ''Hunter, they might shoot.''

''Get down,'' he said, determined not to stop.

Familiar hopped onto Sylvie's lap and patted her shoulder, as if urging her to get down.

''Listen to Familiar,'' Hunter said. ''Get down.''

He kept his eyes on the police. They were slowing more, but so far they weren't making an attempt to block the road.

''Be careful,'' Sylvie cautioned him, her gaze riveted on the patrol cars.

Hunter eased off the gas. He wasn't prepared when the first car whipped across the road. He reacted instantly, though, pressing the gas and cutting the wheel so that the Volvo skidded sideways, barely missing a stand of leafless sycamores on the side of the road.

Hunter turned the wheel back just in time, correcting the car's skid and putting him past the police car that blocked his way.

The road was open before him and he pressed the accelerator with firm resolve.

''Go!'' Sylvie agreed. ''You've got it! Go!''

And he did—as fast as he could drive.

Chapter Fifteen

Hunter had grown up on the island of Manhattan, and he knew it well. That knowledge served him in good stead as he whipped the Volvo down the streets, cutting and winding through little-traversed streets as he made his way back to midtown. As he drove he told Sylvie about the woman he'd followed to the entrance of Candlewick.

"It was dark in the bar. I didn't get a really good look at her, but I'm sure she was wearing a wig. The glasses were big and dark. I didn't really see her eyes. She had a good figure, and she wasn't trying to hide that." He glanced at Sylvie.

Sylvie sat silently beside him, her face pale and her gaze concentrated on the road. She had stopped shivering, but her skin was still translucent. And her blue eyes were enormous, as if she were seeing something other than the cityscape.

"She could have been anybody, but she went to Candlewick. And the guard seemed to know her. That's all I saw before I went past. Maybe Alice saw something more."

"We'll ask her," Sylvie said, but her voice was distant. Hunter was very worried about her.

The cat, too, was unusually silent. He was snuggled on her lap, and Hunter was glad of the comfort Familiar gave her.

"It's going to be okay," he said. "We have to find Bobby and get the doll. Then I'll turn myself in to the police. Once we're sure the children are safe, I'll do whatever it takes to clear this mess up. They don't have to know you played a role in this at all."

Sylvie's smile was wry. "I'm not afraid of the police," she said.

"What's wrong?" He thought again of the packed suitcase. It was too much for her. She was going to run. And he didn't blame her, he thought as he felt that familiar emptiness in the pit of his stomach. He didn't blame her at all.

"This is all too much of a convenient snarl," she answered.

"What?"

Sylvie stroked the cat, who sat up on her lap and put a paw on her mouth, gently pulling at her bottom lip.

"There's something I have to tell you, Hunter."

It was the tone of her voice more than her words that heightened his sense of foreboding. "Sylvie, you can tell me anything."

She finally looked at him, and the look of pain in her eyes almost made him forget he was driving. Only when the cat growled did he refocus his attention on the road. There was no sign of the cops, and he slowed considerably. "Whatever it is, just tell me."

"One of the men I saw last night, after I followed the delivery man. I know him."

Hunter gave himself a moment to digest the words.

"How do you mean you know him?" He tried to keep the question casual, but he could hear the tension in his voice.

"I was going to marry him."

It was the unexpectedness of the confession that made his hands tighten on the steering wheel.

"Someone you were going to marry is involved in this blackmail scheme?" He didn't believe it—it wasn't possible that in a city of millions, one of Sylvie's romantic encounters should just happen to be involved in a scheme to ruin him.

Sylvie turned away and looked out the window. "Chester said you would understand, but I knew you wouldn't."

Hunter couldn't explain the rush of anger. He was suddenly, hotly furious. "You told Chester Fenton this, a man you don't even know, before you told me?"

Sylvie didn't look at him or answer.

"I thought we had an—" he stumbled. He wasn't certain what he thought they had. Not an agreement or understanding. Something deeper. A partnership. "I thought we were working on this together," he said.

Sylvie finally looked at him. There was no expression on her face. Her blue eyes were dull and flat.

"His name is Augie Marcel. I met him when I was living in St. Mary's Orphanage. He offered me something I hadn't known in years, a connection to another person. He made me feel special. He wanted to marry me and start a family. I was seventeen, and I was terrified that I would spend the rest of my life alone, one of the many unwanted people.'' Her voice broke and she turned back to the window.

Hunter knew how much it cost her to reveal her past so blatantly, yet he couldn't move beyond the anger that held his hands bonded to the steering wheel. He'd been living in some fantasy where Sylvie West had miraculously dropped into his life. She'd been a gift from the gods, a woman he had begun to view as a partner.

And now she was telling him she "knew" one of the men involved in the blackmail scheme that threatened to ruin not just his career, but a child's life. If a child died because of his doll—no matter that he wasn't responsible for the toxic substance—he would always hold himself responsible.

"You knew him?" He waited, but she didn't respond. The image of her packed suitcase came back to him. "So what, exactly, is your relationship with this Augie Marcel?" He sounded as cold as a professional prosecutor. And he was glad.

"I told you. I knew him a long time ago. I just saw him when he was going into that building."

Hunter was struck by another even more bitter thought. Sylvie wasn't running away from him, she was running to this Augie Marcel. It made good sense that she wouldn't go alone. Now that she'd revealed Augie Marcel, a lot of puzzle pieces were falling into place.

Hunter felt the touch of her fingers, a featherweight.

"Hunter, I haven't seen Augie since I was eighteen."

He looked at her and found that his anger had burned up any compassion he might have felt toward her. "How did you manage to be the one person in the store stocking those shelves? If I hadn't grabbed you, would you have thrown yourself into my van?"

"Hunter, that's not the way—"

"Don't bother, Sylvie. I've got a really clear picture of what's been going on. No wonder the black-mailers have been able to calculate my every move. I have to say, it was pretty ingenious for them to put someone behind my line of defense."

"I'm not working with them." Sylvie's voice had grown calm and emotionless.

"Was it part of the plan for you to sleep with me, or was that just a little something extra you threw in?"

Sylvie's hand came at him, catching him sharply on the side of the face. Though it stung, it was nothing compared to the rotten way he felt.

He was completely unprepared when she grabbed at the door handle and opened the door. The car was still moving at a brisk pace.

"Meow!" Familiar tried to push her hand away from the latch, but she ignored the cat. She pushed him aside.

Hunter made a grab for her as he slammed on brakes and swerved the car against the curb. She was going to climb out of the car even if it was moving.

"Wait a minute," he said, trying to grab hold of the door handle.

"Don't touch me," she said, hitting the door with her hip and forcing it open. She turned to him. "You're right. I was in this up to my ears. It's the way I was brought up, to scrabble to survive. Whatever It Takes—that's the motto of survival out in the big bad world. So now you know the truth. Consider yourself lucky, Hunter. I'm out of your life.'' She jumped to the sidewalk and started walking.

Hunter sat in the car, numbed by her sudden confession. She was marching down the street, but it wasn't much of a stride. Her boots had been ruined by the snow, and she was limping.

Regret rose instantly in Hunter's heart. His hand was on the door handle, but he stopped. It was better this way. He looked around and realized that the neighborhood she'd gotten out in was a rough one. But, hell, she'd grown up in worse and had learned the tricks of survival. She'd said as much.

A few of them she'd learned really well.

But he couldn't just leave her here.

''Meow!'' Familiar set up a howl. Then he jumped on Hunter, batting him on the face with his sheathed claws. ''Meow!''

Hunter rubbed the cat. ''Betrayal is the one thing I can't forgive. A little boy's life is still at stake here.''

He started the car and pulled back into the traffic, intending to go after Sylvie. He hadn't made it half a block before the cell phone at his hip began to chir. He knew it was the blackmailers.

They'd finally decided to tell him where to leave the formula. He checked his watch as he answered. Nine o'clock.

''Hunter Semmes,'' he said slowly.

''We've been looking for you. If you think you have any tricks up your sleeve, think about this.''

Hunter wasn't prepared for the wail that issued from the phone. ''No, no, no!'' A young boy cried. ''Stop!''

The man's voice came back on. ''Listen and listen

good. You've got one chance to do this right. And don't call the cops. If we see any cops, the boy's not going to wake up to find what Santa brought him."

"Threats aren't necessary. I intend to give you the formula," Hunter said. "But the boy is to be set free before I give you anything."

"You aren't giving the orders here. Let's not forget that," the man said angrily. "Be at the ice-skating rink at Central Park. The west side of the rink. A man will approach you. He'll have the doll. You'd better have the formula. Just hand it over. He'll give you the doll. The boy will be returned home after we verify the formula."

"That could take hours!" Hunter didn't like that condition.

"It could. That's why you've got less than an hour to be at the skating rink. Make it fast, Dr. Semmes."

"I can't possibly—I have to go and get the formula. That's across town."

"You'd better hurry, then."

The phone went dead in Hunter's hand.

SYLVIE JUST KEPT WALKING. She didn't know where she was, and she didn't care. She just wanted to get as far away from Hunter Semmes as she could.

As mad as she was at Hunter, she was even more furious with herself.

She'd known what his reaction would be. Again and again she'd been taught the rules of real life. Yet she'd foolishly hoped that she could tell him the truth. She'd wanted so desperately for Hunter to be the one who made her believe in love.

"In stupid fairy tales," she muttered darkly as she turned a corner.

Augie Marcel wasn't the only coincidence in the whole sordid mess. What about Connie? Sylvie kicked at a can in the snow and almost fell down when her boot slipped.

Hunter's ex had turned up at the store, very conveniently. But Sylvie hadn't jumped to any untoward conclusions. And Connie had said she'd been talking to Hunter.

Sylvie hadn't spoken to Augie Marcel in years.

But Hunter hadn't even given her a chance to explain. He'd immediately thought the worst. He knew just enough about her background to assume that she was bad.

Well, he could just go to hell in a handbasket. She was probably fired, but the least she could do would be to make an appearance and try to hang on to her job. She stopped, suddenly worried about where she was.

She'd paid no attention to directions, and when she finally did look up, she felt her heart drop to her stomach. Three men in worn jeans and leather jackets were leaning against the wall of an abandoned building. They were watching her like hungry dogs. One of them laughed.

The sound was chilling. Sylvie had an almost undeniable impulse to run. But she knew better. Running would only put them on her, like dogs after a cat.

She held her ground and pretended to ignore them.

"Hey, little Christmas helper," one of them called out while the other two laughed.

Sylvie wished that she'd burned the elf suits. She wished she could punch Hunter Semmes in the jaw. She even wished she hadn't gotten out of the car without knowing how to get home. The only thing to do was brazen past them, pretending she wasn't afraid.

She continued walking, cursing the boots that made her look vulnerable.

"Hey, sweetie," one of the men said as he pushed off the wall and stepped to block her path. "Are you lost?"

She meant to keep walking, but she hesitated, and in the split second, she saw that he knew she was afraid. Even if they didn't intend to harm her, they were going to have some sport.

"She looks like she got lost from the North Pole," one of the others said. "Hard to find a subway route there, isn't it?"

They all laughed, and Sylvie tried a tiny smile. "Merry Christmas," she said, stepping to the side to avoid the man.

"It could be a lot merrier if I knew an elf like you," the one blocking her path said as he reached out a hand and grasped her arm. "And I was just telling my friends that I didn't believe in Christmas."

Sylvie had a wild impulse to run, but that would be the absolute worst thing she could do. She stood there, not trying to pull away from his touch. "I'm late for work," she said reasonably. "You know, work, where you perform a job and they give you a paycheck." She put just the right touch of sarcasm in it.

"Oh, the little elf has a sharp edge to her," the man said, tightening his grip. "An elf with a bit of spirit in her. This could make the holidays very exciting."

IN ALL MY MYSTERY-SOLVING days I've never seen a man more hardheaded. He can't just drive off and leave Sylvie in that part of town. But I can't stop him.

So, it's up to me. Let's see, here's the switch to the window. There it goes, down all the way, and now a leap to freedom. I only hope the snow is softer than it looks.

One long kitty leap, a tumble, and I'm on my feet. Nothing broken, thank goodness. But I've got to make some tracks. Sylvie could be in danger right this minute.

I'll deal with the headstrong Dr. Semmes at a later date. He's going to have to learn some hard lessons before this is over. I only hope Sylvie isn't the one who pays the price for them.

HUNTER MADE A FUTILE grab for the cat. But Familiar was out the window before he could stop him. He slowed the car to the blare of horns behind him and watched as the cat tumbled, leaped to his feet and disappeared along the sidewalk.

Regret over his actions was instantaneous. He'd been wrong to let Sylvie out of the car. Wronger than he'd been about anything else in his life.

And knowing it didn't lessen his regret. But he had no time to go back and look for Sylvie. If he was going to make the appointment at Central Park, he could only keep going and trust that Familiar would take care of Sylvie.

He eased down on the gas and headed toward his home as fast as he could drive.

SYLVIE TOOK A DEEP BREATH and looked around. The street was still empty. This wasn't the kind of neighborhood where people woke up to fresh-brewed coffee and the morning newspaper with a kiss for their spouse and kids. Many of the run-down apartments were occupied only by rodents and the homeless. Her anger had led her into a trap.

"Listen, I'm late for work. I know this is fun for you, but I have things to do." She tried to step back, but the man kept his hand on her arm.

"You're right. You've got plenty of things to do." He grinned at her, and Sylvie thought of a predator, something very hungry, eagerly looking at its next meal.

"Don't make trouble for yourself," she said calmly. "I'm going to turn around and walk away from this. It's not too late to pretend this didn't happen."

"Honey, I think you've got it wrong. You're the one in trouble."

She felt her spine tighten. She was in trouble, and it was her own stupid fault.

"I live right up the block," the man said. "How about a little Christmas visit. Santa hasn't been very kind to me in the past."

"Take your hand off me," Sylvie said, backing up another step.

"Oh, you're frightening the elf," one of the other men said, chuckling. "Don't scare her off."

"She's not going anywhere," the one who held her answered.

Sylvie caught a sudden movement out of the corner of her eye. To her complete astonishment, Chester Fenton, dressed in his tweed suit with his umbrella, turned the corner and headed her way. He walked with a jaunty stride, swinging the umbrella as if he were out for a stroll in the park.

When he saw the scenario in front of him, he stopped. His happy smile disappeared and he strode forward.

"Take your hand off her," he said in a voice that crackled with authority.

"Hey, old man, beat it." One of the men against the wall stepped in front of him.

In a movement that was a blur, Chester jabbed him hard in the stomach with the point of the umbrella. It was a move so hard and fast the man went down, gasping for breath, in less than ten seconds.

Chester pointed the umbrella at the second man. "I have some of that for you," he said. "Come right on."

The man reached in his pocket and pulled out a knife. In the sudden silence, the blade made a loud click as he whipped it open.

Chapter Sixteen

The morning sun glinted on the wicked edge of the knife blade. Sylvie felt as if she'd stepped onto a movie set, only it wouldn't be fake blood. The toughs confronting them were real villains, not actors, and Chester, no matter what he thought, was an older man in his seventies.

"Come on, Grandpa," the knife-wielding man said.

"I'm glad to oblige." Chester leaped forward, the umbrella cutting a swath through the air.

"Chester," Sylvie said softly. "Don't—"

"Nonsense," Chester said. "I've handled their sort before. I may look like a kindly old gentleman, but I've had an interesting life. I took a few lessons from the most renowned fencing master in Vienna." He assumed the stance, left hand in the air as he pointed the umbrella. "Come on, you ruffian. I'll have you eating pavement, too." He advanced forward.

The man holding Sylvie dropped her arm and reached into his jacket. Sylvie saw his knife as he pulled it out. Without thinking, she turned, whirled, and kicked at his hand, sending the blade skittering across the icy sidewalk.

"You'll pay for that," he said coldly, pushing her so hard that she had to cling to a streetlamp to keep from falling.

The man bent down for the knife, and Sylvie saw a black blur that seemed to be propelled by a growl of feline fury.

"Familiar!" Sylvie cried, not believing her eyes. It was the black cat, and he was on the man's head like a demon, claws ripping away.

Only a few feet away Chester delivered a punishing blow to the second man's head. Before he could recover, Chester stabbed him in the ribs three times, battered the other side of his face and stomped on his foot as hard as he could.

"Run for it, Ray. I'm not hanging around here," the man Chester was fighting said, turning and rushing down the street.

"Wait!" The one Familiar rode tried to spin and run, but the cat grabbed his right ear and crunched down with his teeth.

The man shrieked and danced around in a circle. At last Familiar let go, jumped safely away and ran to stand beside Sylvie's feet.

Sylvie watched in grim amusement as two of the men gathered their moaning partner and scurried off.

"Sylvie, are you hurt?" Chester Fenton was instantly at her side.

Although she was breathing hard, she was amazed to see that Chester wasn't even puffing. He looked as pink and rosy as if he'd just stopped for a chat.

"I'm fine," she said, wondering if she really was. The men had frightened her. And her own stupidity was even more upsetting. She could have been seriously injured—or worse—if Chester hadn't come along. And Familiar.

She scooped the cat into her arms and then looked in the direction the cat had come from. Maybe Hunter was on his way, too. Maybe he regretted what he'd said.

But the sidewalk was empty. There was no sign of Hunter. The small hope that had leaped to life inside her fluttered and died. Hunter wasn't coming to look for her. He didn't care what happened to her. Familiar had obviously jumped from the car.

Chester took Sylvie's arm and began to escort her briskly along the sidewalk. "I'm not afraid of this neighborhood, but I don't think we should linger. Just in case they go for reinforcements." He smiled. "What are you doing in this 'neck of the woods' as we used to say when I was a sprout?"

"I could ask the same of you." Sylvie fell into step with him, trying hard not to show her complete emotional turmoil.

"I had some toys to deliver. Christmas is getting very, very close," Chester said. "Not a lot of time left. So where is the good doctor?" Chester stopped and looked around as if he'd just noticed that Hunter wasn't with her.

"Hunter is, uh, he's…" Sylvie had to stop because of the lump in her throat. Of all things—she was about to cry.

"My dear," Chester said, putting an arm around her. "What's wrong?"

"I told Hunter about Augie. You were wrong, Chester. He thought I was involved. He didn't even really give me a chance to explain. He jumped to the conclusion that somehow I was to blame for the blackmail."

"What about the doll? Did he manage to retrieve it?" Chester asked, holding Sylvie close as he urged her to walk on. The black cat was at his side, glancing back behind them.

"They never called him," Sylvie said, remembering how panicked Hunter had been.

"That's not good," Chester said. "Wait here." He left her at the corner as he stepped into the street. Just as he lifted his hand, a cab wheeled around the corner and pulled to a halt. Sylvie looked in both directions. Somehow Chester had managed to get the only free cab in the entire area—it was a miracle.

In a matter of moments she and the old gent were safely inside the vehicle. With its heater on full blast, the taxi sped toward her apartment.

While Chester asked questions, Sylvie recounted their separate adventures at Candlewick and the fact that they'd discovered the identity of the young boy at risk as Bobby Blalock, son of Clarise Blalock.

"I know the family well," Chester said, his forehead furrowed. "Clarise has had a time of it since her husband died. Bobby is an only child. A sweet tot. This is terrible. As soon as I'm certain you're safe in your apartment, I'm going to get in touch with the Blalocks."

"I don't think they're home," Sylvie said, repeating what the guard had told her. "I'm afraid for that child," she added, and even though she closed her eyes she had a vision of Hunter Semmes. If anything happened to Bobby, she knew Hunter would never forgive himself. "What can we do?" she asked.

Familiar snuggled into her lap and gave her chin a lick.

"The cat has a few ideas," Chester said.

"I don't know where Hunter is. I don't know if he's heard from the blackmailers. I don't even know if Bobby is truly missing." She had a thought that made her sit bolt upright. "Don't take me home, take me to work," she said. "I can find out more stuff at the store."

Chester gave her a long look. "Are you sure, my dear? You've just begun to thaw. I was thinking of a hot bath and a cup of mango tea."

"The store," Sylvie said, giving the driver the address. "I just had a thought. I'm not the only one with recurring romantic interests. Hunter's wife was in KATZ Meow. And Hunter followed a woman from The Jungle Room to that same neighborhood, Candlewick. Want to take any bets that Connie Semmes has some connection with Candlewick? Hunter even said that she took him there once—because she wanted to live in that kind of area."

Sylvie felt as if she'd swallowed a fistful of vitamins. She was suddenly energized. There was a connection between Connie and what was happening in Hunter's life. There had to be.

"That does seem a bit odd," Chester said. "But let me caution you against jumping to conclusions, Sylvie. It's the very thing that Hunter did, and it was wrong of him."

"But I'm right," Sylvie said. She had to be. "And I'm going to prove it and make him eat his words. He thinks because I grew up hard that I'm the one who brought this into his life. Well, I think just the opposite. I think it may very well have come from someone in *his* past.''

She caught the worried look on Chester's face. Even Familiar was looking at her hard. ''What is it?'' she asked.

''Being right isn't always the most important thing with someone you love,'' Chester said gently.

''Meow!'' Familiar nodded at her.

''Being right is very important to me,'' Sylvie answered stubbornly. ''You haven't been accused of being part of a cruel scheme.''

Chester's blue eyes held sadness. ''The important thing is making sure the child isn't injured. And in allowing Hunter's dolls to be distributed so that children all over the world can lead safer lives. Don't lose sight of that.''

Sylvie bit her bottom lip. ''You're right,'' she said.

Chester patted her arm as the cab pulled in front of KATZ Meow. ''Be careful, dear. I'll be in touch.''

''Meow!'' Familiar agreed.

''Where are you going?'' Sylvie asked as she got out of the cab. She leaned in the door.

''Familiar told me he was interested in something to eat, and then we're going to try and find Hunter.''

''How?'' Sylvie asked. ''He could be anywhere.''

''We could use magic,'' Chester said, the twinkle back in his eye. ''Or we could use the telephone. You said he'd forwarded his calls to his cell phone.'' He laughed at the expression on her face. ''For an old codger, I do enjoy this new technology. Why don't you call him, too?''

Sylvie shook her head, backing away from the vehicle. ''No. I won't be calling him.''

Chester arched his eyebrows. ''Then I'll call you.

To check and see what you've discovered. It might prove useful.''

"So you think I'm right.'' Sylvie felt another rush of energy.

"You could be. If you are, it would explain a lot of things that have been troubling me. But off you go, and please give Alice my regards. She is a remarkable woman. I've never tasted such delicious cranberry pudding.'' Chester tapped the partition on the cab. "Drive on, my man.''

Sylvie watched as they pulled away from the curb. She knew she looked a wreck, but it didn't matter. Chances were that she was fired, anyway. But she might get one more chance to work on the store computers. She wanted a couple of things, but the most important was Connie Semmes's address. It would be easy enough to access, if she could find Connie's credit card charge slip.

ONE DISASTER AVERTED and now the promise of food. In a city that never sleeps, one would think that there would be good food available everywhere. I think I've lost at least two pounds since I took over this case. Thank goodness for Chester, who appreciates that a cat works up an appetite while fighting the forces of evil.

Let's see, we're getting out. This isn't exactly Tavern on the Green, but I think we can grab a hot dog from the vendor here. And Chester wants to use the pay phone.

I'll munch my dog while he tries to locate Hunter. I hope he thinks to get chili. It isn't my normal gourmet fare, but it'll suffice for the moment. The concept of a cat munching a dog in the middle of New York

City is one that gives me great pleasure. If I had time to pursue my artistic talents, I'd paint something to this effect. Maybe in the impressionistic mode. Something to consider for retirement, I suppose. Of course, if I don't improve my diet, I won't live long enough to retire.

I hadn't intended to stay in the city for so long. Truth be told, I'd like nothing better than to catch a flight out of here tonight and make it home for Christmas. I never intended to miss snuggling beneath the mistletoe with Clotilde on this wintry holiday.

I'm glad my romantic life is less topsy-turvy than the humanoids'. Look at all the work Chester and I have put into Hunter and Sylvie. Yet they persist in making a muddle of everything. Hunter has a good point about Augie Marcel, but Sylvie is equally correct in suspecting Connie Semmes. So why can't they simply compare notes and investigate? Instead of accusing each other, they should be concentrating on the facts, digging up the truth.

Logic! Humanoids are devoid of it. My, that was almost a rhyme. Perhaps if not painting, I could take up poetry in my old age. I suppose I should feast my eyes on the city and take a few mental notes so I'll have something to write about later.

But tonight is Christmas Eve, and I have my work cut out for me. Sylvie is working on the ex-wife angle. Augie Marcel is also a wild card. Where did he come from? That's the obvious question Sylvie hasn't asked. I think she's afraid of the answer. I suppose I'll have to figure out some way to prompt her.

Ah, Chester has made contact. I'd better gulp this wiener and get ready to rock and roll. It's show time!

HUNTER ANSWERED THE PHONE on the first ring. He had the formula and all of his research material in an envelope on the seat of his car. He was ready for the meeting, but he was short on time. Of all the voices he expected, it wasn't the cultured tones of Chester Fenton.

"Where are you?" Chester asked.

"Headed for Central Park. It's time to make the delivery. I'm supposed to be at the skating rink, west side." Hunter was compelled to tell someone of the plan, in case things went wrong. "If anything happens, try to—"

"I'm not far away," Chester said, sounding reassuring. "Familiar is with me, and we'll be there as backup. What's the plan?"

"I'll make a clean exchange. I can't risk the child. And if they don't get it this time, they'll do something else." He felt completely defeated. "I can't fight this kind of mentality," he said. There was a pause. "You haven't seen Sylvie, have you?" he finally asked.

"We saw her and helped her out of a bit of trouble." Chester cleared his throat. "Hunter, I don't mean to pry into your personal business, but Sylvie was almost seriously injured."

Hunter turned into the road that bisected the park, nearly swerving into the curb. He was almost at his destination, but his biggest concern now was Sylvie. "What happened?"

Chester told him about the incident. "You should call her," he said. "She went in to work at the toy store. She had an idea that she might be able to find some information for you. Even though she's terribly hurt, she hasn't given up. She's determined to help you.''

''Is it a desire to help or guilt because she's involved?'' Hunter asked bitterly. ''She was going to marry that man. Now he mysteriously reappears in her life—and mine? Chester, she had her clothes packed. She'd even taken everything off the walls. She was leaving. And I think she was going with him.''

''What about your ex-wife, who showed up at KATZ Meow, making it a point to let Sylvie know she was up-to-date with all the developments in your life? Including the dolls? What about the fact that Connie wanted to live in Candlewick?''

Hunter felt as if he'd been punched in the stomach. ''I didn't know— But Connie couldn't be involved in this. She never paid any attention to anything I told her, if I ever even mentioned the dolls. She thought everything I wanted to do with my life was a waste. And why would she bother talking to Sylvie at KATZ Meow? Connie doesn't care what happens in my life.''

''She obviously knows a lot more than you think,'' Chester said.

''How?'' Hunter was perplexed.

''That's a question I'm sure Sylvie has mulled over. The difference is that she didn't jump to the conclusion that you were somehow involved.''

Hunter took a long breath. ''Touché,'' he said softly.

''There is an art to loving another person,'' Chester said in his rich baritone. ''Trust is the most important ingredient. Trust in the other, but most important, trust in your own heart, Hunter. You have to trust your heart.''

''That's a difficult prescription,'' he said, trying for a light note. Chester's wisdom had struck a deep chord. It wasn't Sylvie he didn't trust. It was his own judgment.

''It's not hard at all, if you believe in miracles,'' Chester said. ''Now call that young woman this minute. Familiar and I are on the way. We'll keep an eye on things, and no one will ever suspect an elderly man and a black cat.''

''Thanks,'' Hunter said, feeling a rush of eagerness at the thought of hearing Sylvie's voice. He'd been wrong to accuse her, very wrong. An apology wouldn't undo the damage, the danger he'd put her in, but it was a start toward making things right between them. As soon as he could, he'd call her.

SYLVIE GAVE THE COMPUTER clerk her saddest smile. ''I'm in a lot of trouble,'' she said. ''Look at me. I was almost attacked this morning by three thugs, I'm late for work, and now I think I messed up a charge. I'll be fired for sure if I don't straighten this out.''

''I'm sorry,'' the young woman said with a hint of sympathy. ''I'll try to help you, but I can't let you use the computer. Tell me the name of the customer, and I'll look her up.''

This wasn't going the way Sylvie needed it to go. Who would have thought the clerk would be the helpful type? ''The problem is, if you help me, then you're involved.'' The clerk nodded. ''But if you took a coffee break, and I slipped in here, then no one could come back on you if things went wrong.'' She could see the girl wanted to help her, and she felt guilty at using her in such a fashion. But there was too much at stake. She had to get into that computer—and she didn't want anyone knowing what she was up to.

"What, exactly, is it you need?" the girl glanced at the closed door of her office and then at her watch.

"An address. All I want to do is call the customer, explain the mistake and make it right. I'm willing to pay the difference out of my own pocket. I just need to get it fixed without a formal complaint against me." She felt like a heel, but she pulled out all the stops. "I need this job. I'm desperate."

The young clerk slowly stood up. "I'll take a coffee break. You've got fifteen minutes. If someone catches you, I'm going to say I didn't know anything about this."

"Perfect," Sylvie said, sliding into the chair before the girl had even moved away from the computer.

It took only a few moments to access the charges for the day Connie Semmes had been in the store. With the credit card transaction, she found the address she sought. Her heartbeat increased as she read the location: 224 Candlewick Lane. Her hunch had been right. Connie Semmes had to be a part of what was happening to Hunter. It was easy to figure that the Blalock boy had become involved because of proximity. It all made perfectly awful sense.

She closed out the computer screen and slipped out of the office, making a beeline for the checkout counter where she should have been working.

Alice saw her before she'd cleared the escalator.

"Lord a'mercy," Alice declared, running her gaze up and down her. "What happened to you?"

"I was mugged," Sylvie said. "Well, sort of. But I'm fine. Chester and Familiar saw to that."

Alice's face registered horror. "Honey, you look as if the cats dragged you in. And the floor manager has been looking for you. He's angry. You're more than an hour late, and he's not going to like the way you're looking."

Sylvie shook her head. "I can't help it. I've got to go."

"They're going to fire you," Alice warned.

Sylvie hugged her friend. "So much has happened. I'll fill you in on it all. I just wanted—"

The telephone at the counter rang twice, signaling an outside line. Sylvie felt her heart squeeze. She wanted it to be Hunter. Even though she knew it wasn't, that he was out of her life. The irrational hope that it was him made her heart accelerate.

Alice picked up the line, her gaze shifting to Sylvie. She held out the phone. "It's for you," she said with a smile.

Sylvie took the receiver and spoke into it.

"There's no time for a real apology now. I'll make you one you'll never forget if you give me the chance."

Hunter's voice was the best thing Sylvie had ever heard. She'd intended to stay mad at him the rest of her life. No matter her intentions, she felt her heart melting.

"Are you okay?" she asked.

"I'm at the exchange point. I can't talk long. I just wanted you to know that...that I love you."

She gripped the phone and held it, amazed at the rush of emotion that threatened to overwhelm her. "I love you, too," she whispered. "Where are you?"

"Central Park. Skating rink. I've got two minutes before the exchange. I have to go."

"I'm on my way," Sylvie said. "I have some important news."

"Wait for me at my place," Hunter instructed. "I'll give them the formula, but this isn't over. Just stay at my place where it's safe."

"I can't," Sylvie said, determined to make Hunter believe the evidence she'd turned up. "Hunter, it's Connie. She's behind this. I'm positive."

"Sylvie, my ex-wife is—"

Sylvie didn't give him a chance to defend her. "You just have to trust me on this." Sylvie knew she had to get moving. "Listen to me. Connie came in the store and she knew all about us. She warned me. Then I found out she lives at Candlewick. She—" Sylvia heard several clicks on the line and then an odd buzzing. "Hunter? Hunter, are you there?"

The line was dead.

Chapter Seventeen

"You've solved the mystery," Alice said, grabbing Sylvie's arm. "So it's the ex-wife."

"She's involved," Sylvie said with certainty. "I just don't know how deeply, but I intend to find out." Sylvie gave her friend a quick hug. "I have to go." The disconnection with Hunter had her extremely worried. It could have been a technology glitch—or it could mean something much worse.

"But—"

Before Alice could offer the protest she'd started, Sylvie took off with a wave and an "I'll be back soon!" She wasn't that far from Central Park. On the way past a Batman display she grabbed a pair of black sneakers that looked as if they'd been designed for space flight. If she was going to be any help at all, she needed to be able to run. The shoes were essential—and she *would* pay for them later. But she knew that as soon as she went out the door with them, all hell was going to break loose. Perhaps it would be a good thing if the security cops chased her over to the park.

She took a moment to slip on the shoes and tie them, gathering herself for the escape. She hit the door at a full run and as soon as she did, the theft alarm was activated. With whirs and clangs going off behind her, Sylvie ran into the street and took a left.

She'd gained considerable momentum and turned right at the next corner, running full tilt. She didn't see the broad-chested man who stepped out of a dark doorway. She didn't have time to stop when her brain registered that a crash was imminent. Sylvie hit him so hard that it almost knocked them both down.

"I'm sorry," she mumbled, shaking her head to clear the dizziness as she caught her balance. "I'm sorry." She started forward again. She didn't have time to stop, and she didn't even look up.

A large hand covered her shoulder.

"Not so fast."

The voice was almost familiar. She looked up and felt as if someone had turned off the blood to her heart. The man holding her was Augie Marcel. He was older, more rugged, but the same man she'd almost married. The look on his face was victorious, as if some long-awaited goal had finally come within his grasp.

"Where are you going in such a rush?" he asked. "I've been waiting for you."

It was his grin that made her realize how truly afraid of him she was.

HUNTER CHECKED HIS WATCH. Even if he was fast, the appointed time for the exchange had come and gone. It was ten-fifteen. He stood on the west side of the skating rink and pretended to watch the children and adults who skated past. It was a scene right out of a Christmas card, with the new blanket of white snow all around and the bright jackets, hats, scarves and mittens of the skaters. They circled the ice with varying degrees of expertise, and the air was filled with their laughter.

He was reminded for a split second of Brad's first skating adventure. It had been right at this rink. He and Connie had taken the boy. Brad had loved it—even when he fell, which was about twenty times. Even Connie had laughed as she ended up on the ice.

Connie.

He thought of his ex-wife and the accusation Sylvie had made. His first reaction had been total rejection of Sylvie's charge, but he was long past that now. At one time he might have thought that Sylvie was getting even with him for his rash accusation about the man from her past. But Chester had set his mind to thinking.

Connie had never shown enough interest in his work to even know he was developing a doll. He could have been breeding elephants in his toy shop for all she cared. He honestly couldn't recall a single time when she'd asked him about his creations. The image his mind retained of her was her pleasure as she modeled a new dress she'd bought or showed him a new artist she'd discovered on her journeys to art galleries.

Almost as if he'd called her up in his mind, he glanced across the rink and found himself staring straight at Connie. A cool chill traveled down his spine.

She wasn't aware that he was watching her, or at least he didn't think she was. She was wearing a red jacket and she bent down to talk to a small boy. Hunter felt a stab of pain as he watched Connie and the young boy. He was vividly reminded of Brad and the loss of his son. But it did his heart good to see that Connie had gotten over her hurt enough to make friends with another little boy. It was clear from her interaction with the child that she was very fond of him. Strange, though, Hunter didn't recall that Dr. Klepp had children.

Connie's hands efficiently straightened the child's jacket and then she kissed his cheek before she stood up. Hand in hand, they began walking to the north. They were accompanied by another woman. A blonde.

Hunter squinted and tried to bring them into better focus, but they moved in and out among the crowd that constantly changed along the rink wall. The oddity of his wife's appearance at the rink with a child struck Hunter with the force of a hammer. He still clung to the belief that Connie was not involved in the blackmail scheme, but even as he tried to convince himself, he felt his trust crumbling.

No matter what corner he turned, he ran into Connie. And this time she had a little boy. He moved along the rail, trying to get a better look at the threesome as they negotiated the crowds.

He checked his watch. Whoever he was supposed to meet was now twenty minutes late. He had a choice to make. He could stay and wait, or he could follow his ex-wife and play Sylvie's hunch. It was a tough decision.

Checking all around one more time, he left his post and darted along the wall of the rink, determined to get closer to the women and child. He wanted a look at the boy. The child wore a bright yellow toboggan cap, but dark curls escaped on the side. The closer Hunter got, the more his stomach knotted. It couldn't be! It wasn't possible! Hunter gripped the railing. The child looked like Bobby Blalock. The rush of relief almost offset his anger.

Connie leaned down and smiled at the boy, who looked up at her with the simple love of a child. Hunter clenched his fists.

So Bobby was the bait. He'd been expecting to meet a grown man, but he realized he was supposed to see Bobby and follow, away from the crowded rink. Probably to some isolated part of the park where they could do anything they chose without fear of being seen.

Hunter fell in behind them but turned his attention to the blonde. Who was she? No matter how he stared, he couldn't see enough of her to know if he recognized her or not. There was a solution to that problem. He'd chase them down.

He darted away from the rail and started around the rink. He'd gone only a few yards when he became aware of the man following him. His impulse was to turn and confront the man with his fists. Instead, he forced himself to remain calm as he turned around. The tall, thin man was very familiar. It was the man from KATZ Meow, and he held a package wrapped in brown paper.

"I presume that's the formula," the man said, holding out his hand for the packet Hunter still held.

Hunter checked and made sure the thin man had a package. He didn't offer the envelope. "That's the doll?" he asked, indicating the large paper sack.

"It is, and you've seen the boy. He's safe and sound."

"What assurances do I have that he'll stay that way?"

"The boy is insignificant. You know that. He was a convenient pawn. We only wanted the formula."

Hunter wanted to punch the man in the face. "You'd threaten a child for profit?"

The man laughed. "I'm just an employee. I work for a fee. I don't have time for lofty ideals or such." He reached out and took the envelope. He didn't hand the doll to Hunter, he simply dropped it to the ground.

"Nice doing business with you," he said.

"I'd ask who pays your wage, but I'm certain I'll find out soon enough. When the patents are filed in Washington, for sure."

"That's not my problem," he said, shrugging. He narrowed his eyes as he gazed at Hunter. "They told me to tell you not to burn the doll. There's a substance that's toxic in smoke." He made a mocking salute. "Goodbye, Dr. Semmes. It was a pleasure doing business with you."

Hunter looked over at the place where the women and child had been. They were gone. He looked back at the thin man. "If it weren't for risking that child's life, I'd give you the beating you deserve."

"Brave words for a man who can't do anything except talk. Now I'll be taking my leave, too. Let us know if you need investors in any new projects." He gave a sharp laugh and had almost turned away when he stopped in front of a tall, rugged man.

The thin man spoke up. "Augusto, what are you doing here?" He looked at the tall, handsome man who'd appeared out of the crowd like a dark shadow.

"They want me to take it from here," Augie Marcel said. "Now my assistant and I have work to do." He reached behind him and pulled out Sylvie West.

"I believe you know Ms. West?" Augie's eyebrows arched in delight.

Hunter almost didn't believe it. "Sylvie?" he said. She looked as if she'd had a very rough morning. She wouldn't even meet his gaze.

"I'll take that formula," Sylvie said as she grabbed it from the thin man's hand. "I was afraid we weren't going to get this," she said.

"Hey!" The thin man started to object, reaching to snatch the envelope back.

Augie stepped between them. "I told you I had someone on the inside," he said loud enough for Hunter to hear. He put his arm around Sylvie and gave her a squeeze. "Sylvie and I go back a long, long way, don't we, baby?"

UH-OH. THIS IS A PECCADILLO that not even I may be able to fix. Judging from the tableau I spy, it appears that Sylvie is not on the side of the angels. Hunter's face looks as if he's been shot in the gut and left for the buzzards to finish off.

I'm glad Chester is here. I'm sure he'll think of something. But he'd better be fast. Little Bobby Blalock is disappearing. He and the women are headed out of the park. No matter how heartbroken the good doctor is, he simply must gather himself and do what's necessary.

And I suppose the only way to ensure that happening is if I interrupt this ugly little scene. Well, here goes nothing.

SYLVIE KEPT HER GAZE DOWN as Augie had instructed her. She couldn't afford to give away her role—at least not yet. She had the formula in her hands, but they were a long way from being out of the woods. Bobby Blalock was still in danger.

She felt something brush her leg, and she focused on a streak of black moving at the speed of light. Familiar! And the cat was headed directly for Augie Marcel.

"Wait," Sylvie said, making a lunge for the cat. But her fingers caught only the tip of his tail. He was out of her grasp and launching himself at Augie's chest. He hit with an audible thud, knocking the big man backward several steps.

"What the hell?" Augie asked. He reached into his jacket and brought out a gun. "Is that cat rabid?"

"No, he's—" Sylvie never got a chance to finish. Hunter snatched the packaged doll from the ground, grabbed her arm and gave a serious tug as he took off.

"Hey!" Augie and the thin man yelled in unison as they both realized that Hunter had Sylvie *and* the doll and Sylvie had the formula.

"Let me go!" Sylvie ordered Hunter as she tried to put on the brakes.

"Not on your life," he said. "This time I'm not letting go."

He was as good as his word. His hand tightened on hers and he simply forced her along with him as he dashed toward the skating rink.

Chester Fenton stepped out of the crowd, umbrella at the ready. "Go, Hunter!" he cried. "I'll hold them at bay, with Familiar's help!"

Sylvie looked over her shoulder to find Familiar riding the thin man's back. And Chester Fenton, umbrella working as a rapier, had Augie Marcel in retreat. Sylvie couldn't suppress the grin, but she lost it quickly when Hunter gave her arm a tug and almost made her lose her footing.

"Take it easy," she said.

"That's been my problem," Hunter said, increasing the pace. "I've taken it too easy. Not anymore. I'm not giving up on something I want."

"What about Augie Marcel?" Sylvie asked, finding that she was quickly losing her wind. Hunter had set a blistering pace, but she had to know if her reappearance with Augie had shaken his faith in her.

"I don't care about him. I saw my ex-wife with Bobby Blalock. I don't care about her, either. I don't care about anything except getting that boy and making sure you don't run away from me again."

Sylvie thought she might have to sit down and cry. But Hunter had no intention of giving her that option.

"Run faster," he said, hauling on her hand. "I see them."

She looked past him and saw the two women, the boy between them, headed down a trail that looked like a winter wonderland with the fresh white snow. They were moving at a brisk pace, so fast that the little boy was being half carried between the women.

The sight of Bobby disappearing around a bend in the path made Sylvie choke back her emotions. Hunter's trust was the most wonderful thing she'd ever been given, but there wasn't time to revel in it. She put her legs to good use as she started running in earnest.

She and Hunter were closing the distance fast. Sylvie was focused on the women they pursued, and she saw Connie and the other woman glance back over their shoulders. The second woman was vaguely familiar, but Sylvie was far more interested in watching Hunter's ex-wife.

To Sylvie's consternation, she saw a look of perplexity cross Connie Semmes's face as she recognized her ex-husband closing the distance on her. It was almost as if Connie were shocked to see Hunter.

"Hunter!" Connie called out, forehead furrowing into frowns. "What on earth?" She instinctively drew the child against her legs to protect him. "What's wrong?" she demanded.

Hunter didn't bother with an answer, he snatched the child into his arms and handed him off to Sylvie. "Keep him safe," he said.

Sylvie accepted Bobby, cradling him as he began to stiffen with fright. She saw the outrage on Connie's face, but of more concern was the other woman, who'd turned and was running away.

"Hunter!" Sylvie pointed in the direction of the fleeing woman. Whatever role Connie had played in the abduction of Bobby Blalock, Sylvie could tell that she was no threat to the little boy. "We're fine here. Don't let the other one get away," she urged Hunter.

Hunter seemed to briefly assess Connie, then he made a choice and took off after the blonde, who was running full-out.

Connie made no attempt to leave. Instead she turned to Sylvie. "What's this about?" she asked. She seemed to actually look at Sylvie for the first time. "Why, you're Sylvie West from the toy store. What in the world is wrong with Hunter? He's chasing Lila like she's a common thief."

Sylvie stared at Hunter's ex-wife with a sudden realization. Connie Semmes didn't have a clue about what was happening all around her. She was simply a pawn. She wasn't acting innocent—she *was* innocent. Sylvie looked down at the boy she held in her arms. He wasn't talking, but he was following the chase down the path with very interested eyes. "Bobby?" she said softly. "Are you okay?"

"He was just fine until you and Hunter came up and started chasing us," Connie said. She was over her shock, and she was getting angry. "What's the meaning of all this?" She waved down the path to where the other woman was only a few yards ahead of Hunter.

"Where's Mrs. Blalock?" Sylvie countered. Bobby had begun to wiggle in her arms, and she put him on his feet, taking his hand.

"Aruba, if it's any of your business," Connie said with a hint of hauteur.

"She left Bobby with you?"

"I won't stand here and be grilled like some common criminal. If you must know, the Blalocks are my neighbors. I offered to bring Bobby to the park today. I often bring him here. I used to come here with Brad—this actually isn't any of your business," Connie said. "Oh, my." She made a face.

Sylvie looked over Bobby's curls and saw Hunter tackle the long-legged blonde. The woman went down with a whuff, and Hunter snatched her to her feet, twisting her arm behind her back.

"Hunter!" Connie called. "What in the hell are you doing? What's going on?" Panic edged her voice. "I don't understand what's happening," she said miserably.

"Who is that woman?" Sylvie asked.

"Lila Vernon, one of the nurses Hunter used to

work with.'' Tears started in Connie's eyes. ''What's wrong with Hunter? He's known Lila for years. He's hurting her!''

''How well do you know her?'' Sylvie asked. Hunter wasn't being any too gentle, but he wasn't hurting the blonde. He was simply making her walk forward, something she didn't want to do at all.

''I've known Lila for years,'' Connie said. ''She worked with Hunter, and now she's Peyton's surgical nurse. Peyton is the finest pediatric surgeon in the city.''

Sylvie didn't need anyone to tell her that Peyton was Connie's fiancé. And Lila was his nurse. She shook her head. The entire thing was a hall of mirrors. No one played the role she thought they did.

''Where is Peyton?'' Sylvie asked slowly. Bobby was beginning to fret, and she lifted the child to her hip. Although he was a little restless, he seemed fine. The first thing she wanted was for Hunter to examine the boy.

''My fiancé is at his office, of course. Seeing his patients. He's—I'll call him right this minute.'' Connie started digging in her purse and pulled out a cell phone. ''Just wait until he hears about this. He always said Hunter was crazy. Now we have the proof.''

''Don't call him,'' Sylvie said as gently as she could. ''Hunter needs to tell you some things. It would be better if you waited for him.''

''Nonsense. I'll just—''

Hunter came up beside her and took the phone. ''Wait, Connie. I think your friend Lila has something she wants to tell you.''

''You can go to hell,'' Lila Vernon almost spat.

"Tell her, and tell her fast," Hunter ordered Lila. He still held her arm behind her back, and she glared over her shoulder at him.

"I've got nothing to say," she said angrily.

Hunter handed the phone back to Connie. "Call the police," he said. "Tell them to come right now."

"What's going on?" Connie demanded. "If I call the police, I'm sure you'll be the one they arrest. You assaulted Lila."

"I'm afraid your friend and your fiancé have been trying to blackmail me." He edged close enough to Sylvie that his shoulder brushed her. "It's a long story, Connie. I'll be glad to tell you. But first I want to make sure that Bobby is okay."

"He's perfectly fine. Why wouldn't he be?" Connie's voice had risen to a higher pitch. "He's fine. Clarise wouldn't have left him with me if she didn't trust me to take care of him."

"I'll explain it all later," Hunter said. "Just call the police."

Sylvie took the phone gently from Connie's hand and placed the call. "Officer Augie Marcel needs back up," she said, watching Hunter's face. His reaction was exactly the same as hers had been when Augie had told her he'd given up a life of crime and become a law officer.

"We have a lot to discuss," Hunter said.

"A lot," Sylvie agreed.

"Meow!" Familiar darted down the path toward them. He was slightly out of breath but he headed straight for the package Hunter had dropped in the snow as he'd begun to chase Lila Vernon. Familiar jumped on the Buster Bigboy doll and gave a loud cry of victory.

Chapter Eighteen

By the time Sylvie, Hunter, Connie and a protesting Lila Vernon made their way back to the skating rink, Bobby had fallen asleep in Sylvie's arms. She held the child close, his dark curls tickling her chin.

The crowd around the rink was too thick to see through, but Sylvie kept searching for Chester and Augie. Beside her, Connie moved forward, but she seemed to be in a daze.

Bobby stirred, giving a soft sigh of contentment as Sylvie shifted him. The child's absolute trust in her was amazing. Thinking back over her childhood, she wondered if she'd ever trusted anyone so completely. It had always seemed as if she'd been the one responsible for making the other children feel safe and protected. Perhaps it was her lot in life to make others feel secure.

And then she looked at Hunter. He was a man she could trust. One she could put her total faith in. No matter what happened between them in the future, he would never act cruelly or dishonorably.

Hunter seemed to feel her gaze upon him. He kept one hand on Lila's shoulder as he moved her forward, but he turned back to look at Sylvie.

"I couldn't have done this without you," he said.

Sylvie couldn't suppress her smile. She felt as if she'd been given a tremendous gift. Hunter's approval was something to bask in.

A commotion around the rink caught her eye as the sound of sirens seemed to come at them from all directions. Three patrol cars pulled up not fifty yards in front of them, and officers jumped out.

In the middle of the melee, Sylvie made out Chester Fenton. He seemed as debonair as ever, not a hair out of place. Beside him were Augie and the thin man, who wore a pair of cuffs.

"Dr. Semmes," Augie said, coming forward to relieve Hunter of Lila. "Thanks for the good work."

Hunter took the man's measure. "We need to have a talk," he said. "I owe you an apology."

"Consider it accepted." Augie smiled at Hunter and Sylvie. "I made some mistakes early on, but I've worked to correct them. I lost Sylvie because of some bad choices. But I'm married now to a wonderful woman. Our first child is on the way." He checked his watch. "Any minute, as a matter of fact. We're hoping for a Christmas present that not even St. Nick can top."

"Congratulations, Augie." Sylvie gave the officer a big hug. "Life takes some funny twists, doesn't it?"

"That's what makes it interesting."

Augie helped the officers load Lila and her accomplice into one of the cars, along with the Buster Bigboy, which was going to be thoroughly tested for toxic additives. Chester came over to them, his umbrella swinging on his arm.

"I'd say we've done a capital job of cleaning up this mess."

"Only thing left is to find Dr. Peyton Klepp, the mastermind behind the scheme," Augie said. "We've already detained another accomplice, a burly guy." He went over to Connie. "Mrs. Semmes, you're going to have to come with us, also."

Hunter glanced at Sylvie.

She understood instantly what he wanted. Connie was his ex-wife, but she was also a part of his past. Hunter wasn't the kind of man who abandoned people. "Help her if you can," she whispered.

"Is Connie under arrest?" Hunter asked.

"Not at the moment. Our investigation isn't complete, and we'll need to ask her some questions. Whether charges are filed will be up to the prosecutor."

"Is this really necessary?" Hunter pressed.

"I'll go with him," Connie said. "I want to clear this up. I want to explain. The sooner the better. I have a lot of questions myself." She looked at Sylvie, who still held the child. "What about Bobby?"

"I'll take care of him," Sylvie assured her. "And I'll get in touch with Mrs. Blalock."

"She's due back at two o'clock," Connie said. "I know he's in good hands." She walked away and got into one of the patrol cars.

Sylvie watched the expression on Hunter's face. He wasn't a difficult man to read. He felt compassion for his ex-wife, and it was an emotion she was glad to see. "She'll be okay," she said.

"She will," he agreed. "In fact, I think she may be better than she's ever been."

"I think this calls for a celebration," Chester said.

"Hunter, why don't we gather at your house this afternoon and rehash this case. It's been quite an adventure for an old man."

"Sounds like an excellent idea," Hunter said. "Sylvie?"

"That's the best plan I've heard today. I'll call Alice."

"Don't bother," Chester said with a broad smile. "She's leaving KATZ Meow even as we speak."

Sylvie felt a wave of concern. "She's okay, isn't she?"

"Never better. But Alice is working for me now. She's the perfect partner for my future plans. That woman has the courage of a lion and the heart of a kitten."

"Not to mention that she's a whiz in the kitchen," Sylvie said with a laugh.

"That woman can bake," Chester agreed, patting his stomach.

"Let's say four o'clock," Hunter said. "That'll give us time to take Bobby home." He looked around. "Now we'd better all get busy. Where's Familiar?"

Sylvie last remembered seeing the cat when they chased Lila Vernon down. "He was here…" She turned 360 degrees, but there was no sign of him.

"Ah, Familiar had some last-minute business to attend to," Chester said. "I wouldn't worry about him. He has a knack for getting around, even in New York."

"We can't just leave him here," Sylvie protested. The cat had become so much a part of their lives. Central Park was no place to abandon a pet.

"What if I told you that he's perfectly fine? That

I will make certain of it." He put his arm around Sylvie. "Would you be able to trust me?"

Sylvie was nobody's fool. "That is the issue, isn't it? Trust."

"A vital ingredient to living a happy life. Trust, love and faith." He winked at her. "It seems to me you've had a healthy dose of all three lately."

Sylvie felt the laughter rising all the way from her toes. "A healthy dose," she agreed. She went to Hunter and put her hand on his shoulder. "It's all about letting the right people into your life."

"You're right about that," Chester said. "Now I must be off. I'll see you at four, with Alice in tow." He turned to Augie. "Mr. Marcel, you and your wife must also attend. I insist. We want a firsthand account of all the inner details of this nefarious scheme."

"We'll be there," Augie agreed. "Right now I'm getting out of here." He pointed to a swarm of television cameras headed their way. "Dr. Semmes, I think it's time you made an official announcement about your dolls. If there was ever a moment to seize, this is it."

Sylvie squeezed Hunter's arm. "He's right. You're about to become a household word."

"You'll be at my side, won't you?" Hunter asked.

"Wild horses couldn't drag me away." She turned with him to face the cameras.

SYLVIE STOOD ON THE LADDER and reached tall to put the angel on the top of the tree. It was a magnificent blue spruce that towered fourteen feet in Hunter's living room. Somehow Alice had managed to get the tree inside while the rest of them had been at the park.

She'd also been busy decorating, and fresh holly adorned the mantel and the dining room table. The smell of baking cookies filled the air and made Sylvie's stomach growl with anticipation.

"A little to the left." Alice directed Sylvie in the placement of the last ornament.

When Sylvie had the beautiful crystalline angel perfectly perched, she heard the enthusiastic applause of her friends. She looked down into the smiling faces of Alice, Chester, Augie and his very pregnant wife, Marge, and most important, Hunter. His strong hand held the ladder, and he reached up to help her down and into his arms.

"I can't believe we didn't get mistletoe," Alice said, passing around a tray of hand-dipped, home-made chocolates that were filled with nuts.

"Meow." It was a garbled comment, but it was a cat noise, and Sylvie turned to find Familiar standing beside her with a sprig of something green in his mouth.

"Familiar, where have you been?" Sylvie cried.

"Mistletoe!" Alice proclaimed, grabbing it. "Silly feline. It's poisonous for kitties but the perfect thing for those in love." She held the greenery aloft over Sylvie's and Hunter's heads. "This calls for a good, Yuletide kiss."

"Alice," Sylvie said, blushing to her toes. "Not now!"

"Right this minute," Hunter said as he swept her into his arms.

Sylvie thought she would melt on the spot. She forgot that people were watching. She didn't hear the catcalls or the scattered applause. She didn't have room in her mind or heart for anything except Hunter.

It was only when he released her, holding her steady until her legs could support her, that she realized everyone was watching her.

"We must have a toast," Chester said, laughing out loud.

Sylvie nodded, still a little breathless from the kiss—and from the way the rest of the day had gone. It was the kind of happy ending that seemed scripted by Hollywood.

Once the police had arrived and verified that Hunter's dolls were not contaminated, things had begun to happen fast. Stores all over the country were calling for dolls for the last-minute Christmas rush. Hunter had hired a dozen people to help take orders and ship them out to stores in town.

The phones were ringing off the hook, and even representatives of the United Nations and the World Health Organization had been calling to ask about the dolls.

"Here's to Buster and Molly," Chester said, holding up a bottle of champagne. He popped the cork and began to fill glasses for everyone in the room. "It isn't Christmas Eve without a toast."

Sylvie took a glass and held it up. "Here's to friends," she said.

"To the future," Alice said, sending a smile to Chester that made him laugh out loud.

"To Christmas," Chester said, draining his glass.

An insistent knock came at the door. Hunter pulled it open with a flourish. He stopped dead when he saw Connie standing there.

"I came to wish you a Merry Christmas," she said, stepping into the room. A faint flush touched her cheeks, but she met everyone's gaze, lingering longest on Sylvie. "And I came to tell you the truth."

"Join us, Connie," Hunter said, easing her into the room.

"I didn't know anything that was happening," Connie said softly. "It's important to me that all of you believe that."

Sylvie felt a rush of compassion. She knew what it felt like not to be believed. "I know how something like that can happen," she said.

Augie Marcel stepped forward, his arm around his wife's shoulders. "I can add that we never suspected Mrs. Semmes in the scheme. We knew she was being used by Peyton Klepp and Lila Vernon. But she was never a suspect."

Connie turned to Hunter. "There are a lot of things I'd like to say to you, but I won't. I'll simply say that I've spent most of my life worrying about things that really aren't important. I see now that you were always traveling a different path, one that I want to take some time to explore. Hunter, Molly McBright and Buster Bigboy are brilliant creations. You *have* made the world a better place, and I congratulate you."

She looked around at everyone else. "I know you're wondering how a woman could lose a man like Hunter and end up with someone like Peyton Klepp. I have to tell you, I'm wondering the same thing. I can only say that Peyton never let me see his real identity. The face he showed me was greedy, but then so was I." She shrugged.

"This isn't necessary," Sylvie said. "Come and sit down. Have a toast with us. We've all made mistakes. All of us." She looked up at Augie and shook her head. Never in a million years had she guessed that he'd been trying to contact her to tell her that he'd turned his life around. She'd never given him a chance.

"It's necessary for me," Connie said. "After talking with the police, I found out that Peyton and Lila had this scheme cooked up before he began dating me." She bit her lip but continued. "I was a means to an end, obviously."

"Connie—" Hunter tried to intercede.

"No, listen to me. I'd told Lila about the dolls. It's a bitter irony that I paid just enough attention to what you told me that I started this whole mess. Naturally I didn't see their value, but Lila did. I was so busy being mad at you, Hunter, because of Brad's illness. I decided it was because you weren't focused on making money. I never really even looked at what you were doing. But Lila saw the potential. And so did Peyton. They used my key to get in here to try to steal the formula. Originally they were simply going to steal it and then produce their own dolls.

"When that didn't work, they went on to more drastic measures. The only thing I can say is that Bobby was never in any real danger. I hung around the police department long enough that I heard the report on the doll. That particular Buster Bigboy wasn't contaminated with anything. It was all a hoax."

"What about the children who actually got sick?" Hunter asked.

"I know," Connie said. "It's hard to believe that

two people in the medical profession could deliberately make anyone sick. But they did. There was something in the other dolls. Not life threatening, thank goodness.''

"It's a lucky thing," Chester interjected.

"Well, I'd like to bake up a pan of cookies with a helping of something awful for them," Alice said indignantly. "The very idea."

"I didn't know anything about it," Connie said. "I would have called you, Hunter. I would have. I should have known. There were clues everywhere. It was Lila at The Jungle Room, making sure you picked up the photo. You know, I saw her going out in the red wig and I never gave it a second thought."

"I believe you," he said.

Sylvie had a sudden revelation. "It was Lila who was on the store videotape with Bobby."

Connie nodded. "Peyton gave her a lot of time off. Now I know why. She was always with me and Bobby. We often went to KATZ Meow to shop and so that Clarise could see her little boy."

Connie took a deep breath. "I spoke with Clarise and told her everything. Bobby's fine. He wasn't even aware of anything. And Sylvie, you've got a job at KATZ Meow for the rest of your life. Clarise will always be indebted to you for what you did."

Sylvie smiled. "Thanks, Connie."

"Well, that's all I came to say." She turned and walked to the door. "I'm sorry," she said before she pulled it open. "I'm sorry for a lot of things."

"Stay and have some champagne," Sylvie said, going over to her.

"Stay," Hunter said.

Connie looked at the tree. A tiny smile lifted the

corners of her mouth. "Something smells wonderful."

"It's the cookies," Chester said. "Stay and have some. We're going to have a Christmas party right here on Thirty-fourth Street."

"We might even pop some popcorn, string it and finish out that old tree," Alice said. "I think there are some cranberries in the kitchen."

"Cranberries? I've never bought cranberries," Hunter said. "Or popcorn."

Alice got up and walked into the kitchen. In a moment she returned with both cranberries and popcorn. "They were there," she said.

"No time to argue," Chester said quickly. "Let the party begin."

"Show time," Augie said, "before Marge and I have to leave the festivities and head for the hospital."

They were all laughing as Chester poured more champagne.

AH, THE HUMANOIDS ARE BUSY doing the Christmas thing. And thank goodness for that. It seems like a week ago but it was only this morning that I thought Hunter and Sylvie were kaputz forever. Things have turned around nicely. And Alice is going to work for Chester. A nice touch, but a big surprise.

There's something odd about that old man. If I weren't such a cynical cat, I might make a few speculations. But those are better left to the humanoids.

Now while everyone is busy, I can check my stash. Thanks to Chester, I had time for a few last-minute purchases. I got that exquisite Felix clock for Peter. I need to figure out how to wire it so that he doesn't spend hours with each patient. He gets so involved with all of those blasted dogs. I mean, sure, they need medical attention, but not while cats are in the waiting room.

And Eleanor gets a magnificent sphinx necklace designed by Giovichy Magnoir, the creator of the most incredible jewelry honoring the most magnificent of creatures—the feline.

Jordan will love the wind-up kitty that dances to the tune of "Alley Cat." And there are also the chocolate kitty truffles and the kitty cat socks and the pajamas with all kinds of kitties. I also like the Miss Puss doll. What an adorable Persian face. And the clothes—sheer elegance.

And for the kitten of my dreams, a diamond-studded collar for Clotilde. Nothing ostentatious. This is in the best of taste, with her address tag. And a box of liver paté in the shapes of little mice, shrimp and fish. Adorable, and quite tasty, too.

I just don't understand why humanoids enjoy this shopping thing. My pads are worn out. I've been hustled and stomped in the near stampede of desperate shoppers. The stores are a dangerous place to be. This is work.

But it's going to be worth it tomorrow morning when I watch the faces of my little family. And that brings up another problem. Getting home. If only I could click my paws together three times and do the Dorothy thing. Not so lucky.

I'll have to call home, I suppose. And won't they be glad to hear my voice. I'd better get on it while Hunter and Sylvie are busy with their guests. They're going to miss me terribly, you know. But I have a little surprise for them. One nice thing about KATZ

Meow is the work they do in finding homes for stray animals. I was lucky enough to make it to the Christmas event. And what a bundle of joy I discovered.

Hey, there, little fellow. It's Uncle Familiar. Now just stay tucked away for a little longer. And remember, son, it's your duty to train these humans correctly. I've got your vaccination papers and your certificate for neutering right here. And your name, too. Sputnik. Now isn't that just the cat's meow!

You aren't a replacement for me, but you'll do in a pinch. And I have to get home. After all, Christmas comes only once a year.

Here's a bit of grilled tuna, big boy. Gnaw down and take another little nap. Remember, it's your duty to sleep in the daytime and keep them up at night. That's my boy!

So, on to the phone. I'll punch in the home number and wait. One ringie-dingie. Two ringie-dingie. Three— It's Eleanor. And she's gnawing on me a mile a minute about where I've been and how I've worried them. I suppose I'll have to accept a little scolding before she'll calm down long enough to work out my flight arrangements home.

HUNTER SNUGGLED SYLVIE closer to his chest. The lights of the Christmas tree cast red, green, blue and yellow colors on her porcelain skin, and Hunter couldn't resist tracing the multicolored patterns on her warm flesh. He drew with a slow, sensual finger.

"What an incredible day," Sylvie said.

"It was," he agreed. "Can you believe the World Health Organization took all of the dolls that were left? Right at this moment they're being flown to some children."

"Children who'll have a happier Christmas and a safer life because of you," Sylvie said, kissing his cheek and then moving along his jaw until she nibbled at his ear. "But I get the best Christmas present of all. Time with you."

"Time, as in a life sentence?" Hunter teased.

"I couldn't think of a better way to spend my life," Sylvie said.

"Do you mean that?" Hunter tried to keep it light, but he was suddenly dead serious.

"I do," she said. "And I'm not afraid to say it."

"Would you mind if I gave you your Christmas present now?" Hunter asked.

Sylvie sat up. "Hunter, I didn't—I didn't have time. I didn't even think about a present. It's been so long—"

He captured her stricken face in his hands. "I didn't, either." He chuckled softly. "Chester did it."

"Chester?"

"I hate to say it, but he did. And I couldn't have done better myself." He could see that he had her attention. "But, we can wait," he said. "In fact, I think we should wait. It was a bad idea. It was silly of me to think you'd want your present now."

Sylvie caught his shirt. "Don't think you can tease me and get away with it without some trouble."

"Oh, I can," Hunter said with complete assurance. "I'm doing it."

"How about that present?"

"What present?"

"Hunter Semmes, you have three seconds."

"Or what?" he asked.

"Or I'll kiss you to the point that you forget all

about hiding it from me,'' Sylvie said with a glint in her eyes as she made good on her threat.

Desire for Sylvie swept through Hunter, and for a moment he yielded to it. She was everything he'd ever wanted, and more. She believed in him. It was the best present anyone had ever given him.

He gently broke the kiss and reached into his pocket. The jewel case was small, and he watched her face as he extended it to her.

''Hunter,'' she whispered.

''This isn't just a Christmas present,'' he said. ''It's the rest of my life. I want to share it with you, Sylvie. You're a part of it, a part of me. I want to know that you're as committed as I am.''

Sylvie took the box from his hand. Her fingers trembled as she opened the lid. The diamond caught the lights from the Christmas tree and scattered them into a dancing prism.

''It's beautiful,'' she said.

''It's just a ring,'' Hunter said softly, brushing her dark curls back from her face. He lifted her chin so that he could look into her face. ''It's only beautiful if it's on your finger.''

''Are you sure?'' she asked. ''We haven't known each other—''

''Time is the most important thing we have, but I don't need more of it to know my heart. I love you, Sylvie. I love who you are now, who you used to be and who you'll be in the future. I want you beside me, as my wife. Will you marry me?''

''Yes.'' She took the ring out of the box and handed it to him.

Very gently he slipped it on her finger. ''Before

the year is out," he said softly. "I want to go into the new century with you as my wife."

"Yes," she answered, placing her palm against his cheek. "I've always been afraid to dare hope for the kind of love I feel for you. I was afraid to risk my heart. And now I find that no matter how great the risk, I can't resist you. I love you, Hunter."

"Merry Christmas, Sylvie." He leaned toward her as she lifted her lips to meet him.

Chapter Nineteen

Again Sylvie felt tiny pinpricks of stinging pain in her feet and slowly opened her eyes. It was pitch-black outside Hunter's window, a cold, crisp Christmas Eve. She looked at the bedside clock that showed eleven o'clock. In another hour it would be Christmas Day. The diamond on her hand caught the light from the flames in the fireplace and sparkled with a brilliance that made her catch her breath. It was real. She hadn't dreamed it.

The smile spread across her face as she remembered the night that had just passed. She'd been asleep for only an hour. It seemed the prospect of matrimony made Hunter amorous. The idea of marrying the man beside her made her feel many different things. Amorous was only one of them. And so was trusted and secure.

She stretched long, sighing with the unexpectedly delicious turn her life had taken.

The sharp pain in her left foot made her sit up in bed.

She managed not to cry out as the small black kitten jumped on her foot and began to bite and claw with a fury.

"Where did you come from?" she asked, leaning down and scooping the kitten into her arms.

A loud purr was her only answer.

Cuddling the kitten, Sylvie slipped from the bed and went into the living room where the Christmas tree still burned brightly. The lid was off a large box, and Sylvie went toward it. It hadn't been there when she and Hunter had gone to bed.

Kneeling down, she found the adoption certificate for a small black kitten named Sputnik. There was also a note card with only a black paw print.

"Familiar," she whispered, looking around. But she knew he was gone. "He left you for us," she said to the kitten, snuggling it closer. "I suppose you're hungry."

She went to the kitchen and found the remains of some fish. The kitten purred louder and began to eat.

Sylvie watched the small cat in amusement and then lifted the phone. It was late but she wanted to call Alice. There was so much to tell her friend.

She dialed the number and waited. On the fourth ring, the answering service picked up.

"Merry Christmas," Alice's voice said. "Strange as it may seem, I've moved away. I met a man who made an offer I couldn't refuse. I'm happier than I've ever been, and I'll be in touch when you least expect it. If this is Sylvie, Merry Christmas! Love *is* the answer."

Sylvie felt the tears spring to her eyes, but she wasn't sure if they were from happiness or sadness. Alice had left with Chester. She should have seen it coming, and she was glad for the older couple. They were perfect for each other. She only wished Alice had been a little more specific about where she was going.

"It's Christmas Eve, and it seems that everyone is leaving me," she said to the kitten. He finished the fish and came over, jumping onto her bare legs.

"Hey!" she whispered urgently as she captured him and moved him to her arms. "The problem is that everything in my life is changing so fast."

"Meow!" The kitten's voice was tiny yet demanding.

"You know, you remind me of another black feline. I'm wondering if you're going to be as smart as Familiar."

"Meow!" Sputnik wiggled free of her hold, jumped to the floor, bit her ankle and then patted his empty plate.

"I think we're in trouble," Sylvie said. "We," she repeated, amazed at how wonderful one word could make her feel. She went back to the bedroom and looked in on Hunter as he slept, one arm flung on her pillow. "We are definitely in trouble," she said, suddenly hungry for his arms. "And the wonderful thing is that we're in it together."

SLEIGH BELLS RING, *dah-dah-dah-dah-dah, winter wonderland. Even Washington got some of the flaky white stuff—perfect for Christmas. I caught a late flight out of La Guardia, and I'm home in the land of the Beltway Bandits. I must say, I'm glad to be home for the holiday. I've deposited the gifts under the tree, made sure the Santa snacks were in place, had a tiny little sampling of the turkey and dressing. Life is good.*

I think I'll slip over to Clotilde's. If we follow our

Christmas ritual, she'll have a fire going and we can cuddle a bit before the hordes of humanoids come rushing downstairs.

I want to be home when Jordan gets under the tree. She is a small humanoid, but from the first day she was born, she captured my feline heart.

Eleanor and Peter will be a little miffed with me, but they'll get over it. And there's no one in the world who can bake a turkey like Eleanor.

Ah, check those perfect cat prints in the snow. I'll give a little meow to awaken my darling. And there she is. Exquisite. Soft, tricolored, long, supple fur.

"Merry Christmas, Clotilde." *Now excuse me, my fine fans, but even Familiar deserves a little bit of Christmas privacy. I'll just slip inside—what's that? Is it a bird? A plane? No, it's—impossible! But it's something moving through the sky. And I believe it's—no! It couldn't be a sleigh.*

"Merry Christmas, Familiar."

It's Chester Fenton's voice! And who's that giggling with him? It can't be Alice.

"Merry Christmas." Alice's voice rang out through the night.

"Meow!" Familiar called, just as the door opened and the long-haired calico cat stepped out to greet him.

I'll be doggone, to use a choice human expression. I must be overly tired, or someone slipped something into my food on the airplane. Okay, okay. I give up. Cynicism isn't a virtue. I can tell by the look of wonder on Clotilde's face that she believes what she saw.

I only have one thing to say—Merry Christmas to all, and to all a good night.

If you enjoyed what you just read,
then we've got an offer you can't resist!

Take 2 bestselling love stories FREE!

Plus get a FREE surprise gift!

*Get ready for heart-pounding romance
and white-knuckle suspense!*

HARLEQUIN®

I N T R I G U E ®

raises the stakes in a new miniseries

THE McCORD
FAMILY
COUNTDOWN

The McCord family of Texas is in a desperate race against time!

With a killer on the loose and the clock ticking toward midnight, a daughter will indulge in her passion for her bodyguard; a son will come to terms with his past and help a woman with amnesia find hers; an outsider will do anything to save his unborn child and the woman he loves.

With time as the enemy, only love can save them!

#533 STOLEN MOMENTS
B.J. Daniels
October 1999

#537 MEMORIES AT MIDNIGHT
Joanna Wayne
November 1999

#541 EACH PRECIOUS HOUR
Gayle Wilson
December 1999

Available at your favorite retail outlet.

HARLEQUIN®
Makes any time special ™

Visit us at www.romance.net

HICD

EXTRA! EXTRA!

The book all your favorite authors are raving about is finally here!

The 1999 Harlequin and Silhouette coupon book.

Each page is alive with savings that can't be beat!

Getting this incredible coupon book is as easy as 1, 2, 3.

1. During the months of November and December 1999 buy any 2 Harlequin or Silhouette books.

2. Send us your name, address and 2 proofs of purchase (cash receipt) to the address below.

3. Harlequin will send you a coupon book worth $10.00 off future purchases of Harlequin or Silhouette books in 2000.

Send us 3 cash register receipts as proofs of purchase and we will send you 2 coupon books worth a total saving of $20.00 (limit of 2 coupon books per customer).

Saving money has never been this easy.

Please allow 4-6 weeks for delivery. Offer expires December 31, 1999.

I accept your offer! Please send me (a) coupon booklet(s):

Name: _____

Address: _____ City: _____

State/Prov.: _____ Zip/Postal Code: _____

Send your name and address, along with your cash register receipts as proofs of purchase, to:

In the U.S.: Harlequin Books, P.O. Box 9057, Buffalo, N.Y. 14269

In Canada: Harlequin Books, P.O. Box 622, Fort Erie, Ontario L2A 5X3

Order your books and accept this coupon offer through our web site
http://www.romance.net
Valid in U.S. and Canada only.

PHQ4994R